Dr Robert Lee Moore J.P.

*(Photo copyright: Ards and North Down Borough Council)*

# THE MYSTERY OF STRANGFORD LOUGH

## A Tale of Killinchy and the Ards

ROBERT LEE MOORE

Transcribed, compiled (with glossary), edited and introduced
by Philip Robinson

PUBLISHED BY THE ULSTER-SCOTS ACADEMY PRESS FOR THE
ULSTER-SCOTS LANGUAGE SOCIETY

*The Mystery of Strangford Lough* by Robert Lee Moore (1862-1946) was printed (anonymously) as a weekly serialised novel in the *North Down Herald and County Down Independent* in February, March and April 1909, and has been transcribed and edited by Philip Robinson for this first book edition.

Philip Robinson © 2021

ISBN 978-1-8384549-0-6

# ACKNOWLEDGEMENTS

In October 2019, a working group of the Ulster-Scots Academy organised several public workshops on aspects of R L Moore's work on Ulster-Scots as part of the Ballywalter Ulster-Scots Festival. The materials presented were from the archival collections of the Ulster-Scots Language Society, and included his unpublished Ulster-Scots glossary for north Down; transcripts of his Wullie Gunyun stories (1910-1911); and a transcript of his novel *The Mystery of Strangford Lough* (1909). These workshops were facilitated by the Ballywalter Historical Society, under its chairman Billy Carlile in partnership with the Ulster-Scots Language Society, and the sessions were led by Anne Smyth and Philip Robinson. This novel and its companion volumes *The Leevin Tongue* (USAP 2020) and *Wullie Gunyun's Crack Frae Clabber Raw* (USAP 2021) are a direct consequence of this event. The Ulster-Scots Academy's local working group also acknowledges with gratitude the support the Ballywalter Historical Society has given towards the publication costs of these books.

# CONTENTS

# ROBERT LEE MOORE (1862-1946)

Robert Lee Moore was born in 1862 and had completed his medical training in Liverpool by the age of 25. After his marriage to his full cousin Jemima Moore in Belfast in 1889, he established his career-long medical practice (and family home) on the sea-front of Bangor. This was Redcliffe House, later the Redcliffe Hotel, and now the 'Salty Dog' Restaurant and Bar. He built Redcliffe House after buying the site opposite the harbour pier in 1890. Mrs Jemima Moore died in 1900 and in 1906 Dr Moore married again, to Frances Gill of Ambleside in the Lake District.

Dr 'Bob' Moore had been a medical practitioner in the town for over 50 years. He was a Life Governor of Bangor Hospital, with which he had been closely associated from its beginning, and as he was often called to examine intoxicated 'offenders', his name frequently appeared in the local press as a police witness in court. A Unionist in politics, he served on the Bangor Urban Council for two years, and was Council vice-chairman in 1900.

In his youth 'Bob' Moore was a noted association footballer and athlete. He played half-back for the Ulster Football Club, based in east Belfast, and won two international caps in 1887, against Scotland and Wales. His love of sport continued after his marriage and setting up home and medical practice in Bangor. He was a founder member of Bangor Golf Club when it opened in 1903, he became its second President in 1905. A leading member of the old Bangor Bay Sailing Club, he also belonged to the Royal Ulster Yacht Club at Ballyholme.

# ROBERT LEE MOORE

In 1946 Robert Lee Moore was laid to rest at Bangor Abbey at the age of 84, and his obituary in the local press noted:

> "*He had a marked sense of humour and an inexhaustible fund of stories about old Bangor personalities and events, and he was an authority on Co. Down lore and dialect. The collection of Ulster words and phrases was his hobby, and he wrote extensively on the subject.*"

# THE ULSTER-SCOTS WRITINGS OF ROBERT LEE MOORE

When all of R L Moore's writings and word collections are taken together, they represent a highly significant historical record of Ulster-Scots in County Down from the early 1900s. But it is only in the past decade (a century later) that the enormity of this contribution has been uncovered, as he never published any of these works in his own name.

The most spectacular work in this respect was his manuscript collection of 'local' words for a 3,000-word Glossary (with extensive notes on word histories and origins) that has just been published by the Ulster-Scots Academy Press: *The Leevin Tongue: An historical record of Ulster-Scots as a living language in County Down,* by Robert Lee Moore, (transcribed, edited and introduced by Anne Smyth and Philip Robinson, USAP, 2020). Just as James Fenton's *Hamely Tongue* (Ullans Press, 2014) provides a personal record of contemporary Ulster-Scots as the language of hearth, home and farm in County Antrim, so this 'glossary' of R L Moore provides an historical insight into another dimension of our *hamely tongue* – a dynamic *leevin tongue* – an evolving, living language in its own right, co-existing with a myriad of changing linguistic influences but not only a spoken tongue!

If Robert L Moore had left no other legacy but that of a word-collector, he would nevertheless have earned a place as a very significant contributor to the language's linguistic record from the early 20th century. But to this achievement we must add his writings *in* Ulster-Scots. In 1909 he produced this short novel called *The Mystery of Strangford Lough: A Tale of Killinchy and the Ards* that was serialised anonymously in the local press. This 'kailyard' novel was set in the early 1600s and, although narrated in Standard English prose, it featured local characters speaking in rich and accurate Ulster-Scots, giving us an early demonstration of his command of the language. Then between 1904 and 1911 he also penned about 40 short stories that were not *kailyard*, but written completely in contemporary Ulster-Scots. These were individually published under two *nom-de-plumes* in the local press, first as "Duffer Geordie" in 1904, and then as "Wullie Gunyun" in 1910 and 1911. These short stories were intended to be read by an audience conversant with not only the language but also the local current events, politics, religion, characters and culture, and they again demonstrated his complete confidence and competence in this medium. They have now also been collected and published by the Ulster-Scots Academy Press: *Wullie Gunyun's Crack Frae Clabber Raw* by Robert Lee Moore (transcribed, compiled, edited and introduced by Anne Smyth and Philip Robinson, USAP, 2021).

# INTRODUCING
# *THE MYSTERY OF STRANGFORD LOUGH* (1909)

*The Mystery of Strangford Lough* is a ripping historical novel written in traditional Scots *kailyard* ('cabbage-patch') style – the literary tradition whereby, although the cultural setting is a rural lowland Scots one and the speech of the local characters is written in undiluted Scots, the connecting narrative was written entirely in English.

But it is also in its own right a great Gothic romance of murder, mystery, kidnap, smuggling and betrayal, coded documents, of ghosts in the night, haunted rooms and castles. Yet the setting is local. The heroine is Kate Savage, daughter of Philip Savage of Sketrick Castle and niece of Patrick Savage of Portaferry Castle who is betrothed to Hugh de Montgomery of Rosemount Castle at Greyabbey. But these 'main' characters rarely appear, and it is the local families that populate the book and actually 'speak'.

The setting is the Scots-settled land around 'Lough Cowan' (Strangford Lough), and the period is the second generation of that settlement – the 1630s – the very decade that the *Eagle Wing* with its cargo of Presbyterian exiles including Rev. John Livingstone of Killinchy sailed for America, and when Sir Hugh Montgomery 1st Viscount Montgomery of the Great Ardes died at Newtownards. The 'main' characters and the historical framework of this Scottish settlement are gleaned from the pages of the *Montgomery Manuscripts*; *A Description of the Ardes Barony* by William Montgomery in 1701; *Killinchy, or the Days of Livingston*; and *The Ancient and Noble Family of the Savages of the Ardes.*

The locations where the action takes place are along the shores of both sides of Strangford Lough – 'Strongford' town, Killileagh, Ringhaddie Castle, the 'White Rock' at Killinchy, Sketrick Castle, Ardmillan, , the 'Ghaist Hole' at 'Cummer' (Comber), the 'Mercat Cross' at Newton, Rosemount and 'Ballyboley Hill' at Greyabbey, 'Kirk Cubben', Ardkeen, the 'Walter' shore at 'Portneferry' and many other townlands, islands, creeks and waters in between.

R L Moore displays throughout the story a great familiarity with the Lough from a boatman's perspective. He was a keen yachtsman and frequently sailed these waters with his close friend and Bangor Council colleague James Hamilton Savage. It is no coincidence that the heroine of the story is a Kate Savage of Sketrick Castle. But the story also takes us to the French port of St Malo – where again the reader feels that the author must have known this place too.

Of course, there is a close echo in this book of the similar-sounding novel by W G Lyttle: *DaftEddie, or the Smugglers of Strangford Lough: A Tale of Killinchy.* This was deliberate, as W G Lyttle was the former proprietor of the *North Down Herald* where both books were originally serialised. Indeed Moore's friend James H Savage by 1909 was living in 'Mount Herald', Bangor, the former home of W G Lyttle who died in 1896.

Dr. 'Bob' Moore was well-known in Bangor as the town's 'Police Doctor' and as a police witness in court his name frequently appeared in the local press. He had a sense of fun, and in this historical novel, he inserted a caricature of himself as "Dr Corncat" the "leech" of Killyleagh:

# INTRODUCTION

*"Such was Dr. Corncat, who in the troubled times of 1636 and subsequent years played so important a part in the history of Killyleagh. It was he who, during Phelim O'Neill's rebellion in that year in Ulster, whipped the town bailie with his own hands because he refused to drink to the health of the Merry Hearts of Down. It was he who, during those same troublous times, tied the hands of Tom Hannigan of the Teze to the old pump at Balloo crossroads, when Tom rashly asserted that he did not care a fig for 'The Dutchman.' But to our story ..."*

# CHAPTER 1

## THE SMUGGLERS OF THE LOUGH

In the early part of the seventeenth century our story opens. The beginning of that political end was approaching which has contributed in a great measure to make the County of Down what it is at the present day. But it is not on political subjects that our readers will be called upon to dwell. Our story is a story of real life. History is not a portion of it. Save where the history of the times is closely interwoven with the history of the people, we shall introduce no history. God's day and night then were the same as God's day and night now. The people were different. Superstition, lawlessness and daring were scattered broadcast through our land. The manners and customs of our forefathers were primitive. Hypocrisy did not hold such a prominent part as it does in these days of greater refinement. Smuggling was no crime. It was a deed of daring for which the bold man, if caught, was punished: but it was no crime to mislead a revenue officer and leave him in the ditch. It was no sin to land a few bales of tobacco on a lonely shore, or to stow a keg of rum in a dark cave. Such were the peculiarities of the ancestors of the men and women in this district. The manners of the people of whom we write the record must be gleaned from the record when written. After the manner, then of the ordinary writer of romance, we begin thus:—

It was a dark, tempestuous night in midwinter, 16—. It was not a night to be abroad, much less to be at sea. The wind

1

howled and shrieked over the waters of Lough Cuan. Like many a thing else, Lough Cuan* has changed its name. It was subsequently called Lough Coan, or Cowan, and is now commonly called Lough Strangford, taking its present appellation from the town of Strangford at its mouth. We need hardly remind our readers that this lake, or lough, which is very wide in its central part, begins to narrow into what has been called a river opposite Strangford and Portaferry. After rushing with considerable velocity upwards or downwards, according as the tide ebbs or flows, it passes over a dangerous bar. The Bar of Strangford was, at the time of our story, a much more hazardous place for ships than it is at the present day. The perils of smugglers, and others whose occupation necessitated their movements to be made at night, were very great. On this night, it was, indeed, fearful. The waves lashed madly against the opposing rocks, and roared and tossed in the fury of the tempest. The moon in the early part of the evening had shone with brilliancy, but as the night advanced angry clouds obscured her virgin lustre, causing her light to be uncertain, and the darkness to be more felt.

On the northern side of the Strangford River, at the bar, two

---

* Lough Cuan, Coan or Cowan. In his 1683 "Description of ye Ardes Barony", William Montgomery uses the name 'Lough Coan' for Strangford Lough. Strangford town he calls 'Strongfoord', and the 'great flux and reflux of the sea' at the mouth of the lough he calls the 'Strong Ford River'. In the local press the lough was often called "Lough Coan or Cowan" and the latter was used by W G Lyttle in his novel "Daft Eddie, or the Smugglers of Strangford Lough": "*We'll wan'er nae mair by the Shillan hill, Maggie, nor sit at nichts by the big stanes o' Jerusalem. There's a keen breeze frae the sea, an' the waters o' Cowan are swellin'. Rin, Maggie, for A'm ower weak, and tell the boys no till gaun out till the mac'rel the nicht. There's an angry sough aboot the waters an' the gulls are skreghin' ower Cadoo.*"

muffled figures crouched among the rocks. Their movements were suspicious. The spray from the heaving sea drenched them: the roar of the tumbling waters deafened them. They heeded neither the water nor the wind. Their presence there on that wild night foreboded no good. Some mischief was brewing. They were smugglers, behind them, at a distance, might have been observed two others. They also moved forward cautiously, and with difficulty. The latter two were watching the former. They were revenue officers. The situation was exciting.

The men in advance crept out to the very edge of the boiling waves. The men in the rere concealed themselves behind a jutting rook, and waited patiently. There was a sharp cry! A scream, like the cry of a wounded gull, was borne over the waves in one of the pauses of the storm. It was answered by a similar scream at the other end of the bar. Two wounded gulls on such a night as this—what mischief is a-brewing? One of the men in the front, taking a lamp from the fold of his cloak, allowed the glare to show towards the other side of the bar. He was answered by a similar signal. Shortly afterwards a light was observed right out in the great wall of blackness. It approached.

"They'll har'lv be able tae mak' the bar the nicht, Jamey!" said he of the light, speaking into the other's ear.

"Gude help them," said the other, shivering as a blast of more than ordinary fierceness drove the blinding spray against him, and nearly carried him off his legs.

"Ir ye shair thae warhawks ir no stirrin' the nicht?" said the first, Jamey Gordon by name, after a pause of a few minutes.

"Ay, richt shair em A aboot that Wullie Sinclair. They're a' aff tae watch the boys at Skullmartin. The wreckers hae a richt easy wae o' leevin', Jamey: but A canna say A'm in favour o' showin' them fause lichts ———. Gude save us!" as a terrible blast came over the black sea.

3

"Oh, ay, man," said Jamey, "they haenae till rin the risk o' bein' drooned on sic a nicht as this while seekin' an honest leevin' frae the sea."

"Luk, man. luk! Yonner's the licht." As he spoke he pointed out to sea, where a small flash was for a moment visible. The boat displaying the light flew madly on towards the bar. It was a desperate race for life. Would she weather it? The men at each extremity of the bar held the light aloft to guide their fellows on the boat.

The two figures following crept slowly from their refuge behind the rock. Their blunderbusses were in their hands. The priming was carefully guarded against the rain and spray. They would arrest the smugglers, and were prepared to proceed to any extremity. Like death—like the death they held in their hands—they crept silently forward on the unsuspecting victims. The light out towards the sea grew brighter and more distinct as the ship sped nearer to the dangerous bar.

There was a loud explosion from a gun. The man holding the light reeled. His lantern was dashed upon the ground. Then all was darkness.

Let us leave them for a while, and step boldly on board the little barge. She was a small smack, tight and easy as a duck in the water. All hands were upon deck. All eyes were bent upon the lights occasionally gleaming from the shore. Straight between them, could she make it, her path was clear and safe, and the tiny smuggling craft, "The Jack o Lantern," would once more be riding on the bosom of her own loved lough. Walter (or, as he was commonly called, Watty) Martin stood at the wheel, and guided the little craft towards her home.

It was fearful moment. Already they were nearing the fatal bar that roared and surged with awful noise, while the moaning of the "Rowting Well"† smote horribly on their ears. Wave after wave broke mountain high behind them, impelling the frail craft over the black waste. Already the signal lights on each side of the bar were distinctly visible. The men on board heard the report of the gun. They saw the light go out. They knew there was dark work but they were powerless to give aid. There was a flash, a roar, a creaking of timber, and a straining of cordage. The tiny vessel shot over the ridge of water, and scudded down the Strongford River, as it was then called. They pass Portnaferry: and, in a short time, the anchor is cast in a secure anchorage off Ballyhendry Point at the entrance of Lough Coan.

Then a light is shown from the deck of "The Jack o Lantern" for a moment. Immediately a swarm of small boats, from all sides are round the smuggling craft, discharging the usual

---

† Rowting Well: A whirlpool is a 'wheel' rather than a 'well', but this name was taken by Moore from the a transcription error in the 1701 edition of the source he used, as explained in the following chronological dictionary sources: – [1. *'several rocks appear (in the map as I remember they are called Chickens), but in this country called the **Whullans** or **Wheelons**, I suppose from the **wheeling** of the tides'* (1683 Hist., Richard Dobbs 'County Antrim'); — 2. *'a whirle-poole or eddy of the returning Tides, called by the Scotch the **rowling weele** [in 1701 published version of this 'Description' this is: "called (by the Scotts) the **Rowting Well**"] from the Loud Sound it sometimes makes.'* (1683 Hist., William Montgomery 'Description of Ardes Barony'); — 3. *'the **Ranting Wheel**, lying near Quintin Point, very dangerous for Boats, being a kind of Whirl-pool'* (1744 Hist., Walter Harris 'County Down'); — 4. *'Much might be written of this beautiful inlet of the sea It winds among the hills. But its graceful carves, its **rowting wheels**, and its green patches of fairylike islands would far outrun the limits of notice like this'* (1908 Newsp., 'Our Seaside Resorts. Portaferry' in Northern Whig, 6 July 1908)]

contraband articles of that period. In silence they worked until the grey morning dawned. When all the cargo was gone, the little smack, with a crew of five men, apparently wearied fishermen, and nothing else, toiled home to their anchorage at Killyleagh.

Such was the organisation of a smuggling expedition at the time of which we write. With some of its crew we are destined to become better acquainted.

# CHAPTER II

## THE FATAL BARGAIN

The shot from the blunderbuss of the Revenue officer smote upon the ear of the helmsman even above the howling blast. He knew that some misfortune had befallen his trusty band of assistants, but he was powerless to assist. At that moment it required the greatest coolness and the most intrepid seamanship to guide the "Jack o Lantern" over the bar. The shot from the king's man had been timed so as if possible to cause confusion in the signals, so that the smuggling craft might be cast on the shore, but his movements had been too slow. The intrepid sailor at the tiller had taken his bearings from the lights displayed, and as we have seen, succeeded in floating safely into the narrow channel. But the shot was none the less deadly for being delayed. The figure of Willie Sinclair holding up the lighted lantern was a mark too easily seen to be missed. The bullet sped surely on its way. Smugglers and officers then both lay quiet. As well as the flickering light permitted, they watched for the slightest motion. Had either moved while there any light the life of some of them must pay forfeit. It was an anxious moment. In calm, cold blood they awaited an opportunity for dealing death. The fight was of short duration, but determined in its nature.

"Wullie, luk! yonner is yin o' thae warhawks. Wait; the mune's cumin' oot," said Jamey Gordon to his companion.

Without another word they prepared their matchlocks, looked well to the priming, and waited patiently. At last the moon peeped through a rift in the great black heavens. The smugglers caught sight of their foes. The matchlocks blazed simultaneously. By the groan that followed they were satisfied that they had not both missed their aim.

Nature seemed to assist these lawless men. The great black cloud passed on and again the night was dark. Now was the time for them to make good an escape.

In the darkness Jamey Gordon, half-leading, half-carrying his stricken companion, threaded his way towards a place of safety, and as he knew every step of the way, a shelter was soon reached. They left two wounded men bleeding on the rocks, and the tide flowing in rapidly towards the spot where they lay.

The two men, whose motions we have watched, had not gone far until it was apparent that the man addressed as Wullie Sinclair had been seriously, if not mortally injured. With difficulty his companion was enabled to convey him to the house of a cottager at the shore. Here he was placed in bed more dead than alive, and in a short time it became evident that the wound inflicted would prove fatal.

Here we must leave him for the present to follow the movements of Wattie Martin, the smuggler.

The "Jack" now lay at the moorings at Killyleagh, then a small fishing village. Its commander, Walter Martin, was a man well fitted to occupy the position in which we find him. The son of a thriving tradesman in Killyleagh, he had early chosen the sea for his foster-mother, and his restless spirit and headlong daring made his name a kind of bye-word for courage. He was a man of extreme honour, after his kind, though his sense of honour did not prevent him trading in rum or contraband tobacco. In this run he had been very successful, and twenty pounds of good and lawful money would now reward him for the dangers he had passed.

He was sauntering slowly along the old quay whistling, as was his wont, when he espied a fashionable stranger coming towards him. Walter's quick eye soon scanned the stranger, and he at once set him down in his own mind as a revenue officer. Every unknown person was a King's bailiff or a gauger. Not wishing to encounter the stranger, he was endeavouring to pass unnoticed, when the latter accosted him abruptly:

"Rough night, my man, last night!"

"Ay. Sir, rough aneuch. It was weel for us puir fishin' bodies that we were a' in afore it cam' on."

"What kind of fish do you mostly catch here?"

"Weel, that a' depen's upon oor luck, sir: mackerel and her-rin' in the simmer, and we hae a hard time wi' the oysters in the winter."

"Have you been long following this life?" said the stranger.

"Ay, sir; lang aneuch to ken maist folks hereaboot, an' I dinna' tak' you tae be yin o' them. Maybe ye're stappin' at the Castle wi' the young Laird o' Hamilton?"

Having made this pointed remark to soothe the gauger (for such he took him to be), Wattie looked keenly at the stranger and waited his reply. But none came.

"Do you know a man called Martin?" asked the other.

"Ay, mony o' them, the name's common aneuch in this airt. There's 'Lang Tam' and 'Big Johnny'; 'The Fluker,' and 'Auld Robin,' his faither, an' 'Wee Wattie o' the Jack.'"

"It's Wattie I want," said the stranger, "where ran I find him?"

"That a' depen's upon what ye want wae him. Few weel-dressed folks, like yersel' aften ask for him, an' maybe it wud-na' be for his guid tae tell ye."

The stranger produced some coins.

"Na, na, it's no yer siller A want. Honest folk wunnae tell on their neighbours for the like o' that. Pit up yer gould, man."

"I assure you, my good man, it is for his advantage I am asking."

"Are ye no' a gauger, then?"

"No, certainly not."

"An' ye'll gi'e me yer han' it's for Wattie's guid ye are askin'?"

"Certainly," and he held out his hand.

Wattie reached out and caught the delicate hand (which he noticed had lost a finger) in his horny fist, and with his squeeze brought the blood to his temples, then laughing, said—

"Weel, man, ye're speakin' tae the very boy ye're askin' for."

The stranger then told Wattie to follow him at a little distance, and slowly sauntered round the shore. When they had reached a shady spot, he stopped, and waited till Wattie came up.

"I have been told," said the unknown one, "that I can trust you implicitly."

"That ye can," said Wattie, "if there is a gauger lookin' on. I wadnae dae muckle hairm when ane o' them is near han'."

"And I wish to give you the trial," continued the stranger, not heeding Wattie's remarks. "I have a sister who is staying in this neighbourhood for some time. Unfortunately, she has contracted a liking for a man much below her position in society, and I come over here in the hope of eradicating from her mind if possible this unhappy attachment. I found on my arrival here matters much worse than I expected. My advice, my entreaties—nay, my prayers—were in vain. I told her of the sorrow of our mother, and the grief that would rend our father's heart; but why need I delay you by these stories. It is enough to say that she refused to return home, and insisted upon marrying the man who has decoyed her young heart. I have now made up my mind. I shall take her forcibly to our father's home in France, and I wish to obtain your boat to convey us thither."

Wattie at first hesitated. It was a serious undertaking. The stranger saw the hesitation. He knew the other's weakness. He touched that chord in his heart which with most men produces the right note. He pulled from his pocket a number of bright yellow guineas.

"You will make more by this voyage," he said "than you would at the fishing. You need have no fear of detection. There will be nothing contraband on board."

It took all the eloquence of the stranger, and the display of yellow gold, to gain the assent from Wattie. It took more. It took the assurance of the gentleman that the service expected was innocent, to induce that hardy sailor to consent to strike the bargain. The honour of the simple fellow was finer than the other anticipated.

The bargain was, however, finally concluded. It arranged that on that night week Wattie was to have a boat lying off Ardmillan to convey the stranger and his sister to France.

Giving the sturdy sailor five guineas as earnest of the bargain, and adjuring him to the strictest secrecy, the gentleman turned up a bye-path, leaving Wattie Martin to wander homewards by the shore without repeating the operation of grasping the three fingers.

Who was this stranger? Where did he live? Why did he preserve this secrecy? These were questions Wattie strove to answer, but he could come to no satisfactory conclusion. The more he thought of it the less he liked the undertaking. He was on the point of following the stranger and receding from his bargain. He would return the money, and have nothing to do with the business. He feared it. He who feared neither the terrors of the elements, nor the clutches of the law. He was afraid of the agreement he had made. He knew not where it would end. But the guineas in his pocket chained him with a chain of gold. In no enviable frame of mind he strode leisurely back by the hill bordering the shores of Lough Coan.

Better, far better, had it been that the sturdy sailor had

obeyed the dictates of his conscience. The waves leaped at him, and curled their crests urging him to return. The sun glowed blood-red on the water, but he understood not the warning. The black day was approaching that tinged the fair waters of Lough Coan with a gory red. Like a frail boat in the current of the dreaded maelstrom, he had no power of escape. He must meet his fate steadily, although death stared him in the face. It was too late now!

# CHAPTER III

## THE END OF WILLIE SINCLAIR

For the season of the year, the day was bright and mild. The hoar frost glistened in the sun and sparkled like a bridal veil. The mild clearness of the summer visited once more the icebound earth. The sunbeams danced upon the wavelets that lapped the pebbles on the shore. It was a summer day in winter.

A young girl stood upon the shore of the lough a short distance from the romantic Castle of Ringhaddie. One arm reposed gracefully behind her back. With the other hand she shaded her eyes, as she gazed over the dark blue waters. The background of this picture was the undulating hills of Killinchy. A more comely figure it would have been difficult to find.

Presently her dark eyes lighted up with animation, and taking a bright handkerchief from her pocket, she waved it as a signal to someone out at sea.

Let us follow her gaze. She sees only a little boat, with sails set, making for the spot on which she stands. Only a little boat! Yet it contains all that is left to her in the world. It is her father's boat returning from the fishing. Only a fisher's daughter waiting the return of her father. As seen against the blue waters on the lough, a beautiful picture!

Kitty Sinclair was her father's only child. One by one he had laid his dear ones in the old meeting-house green at Killinchy. His Kitty was his all in all. They lived together in that cottage—now four ivy-coloured walls within a few yards of where she stood. They had lived, here for some years—father and daughter, rejoicing in each other's love.

Many a time had she endeavoured to entice him to leave the society of these lawless men and to settle down to quieter pursuits. But the lawlessness had its charm. On this point he did not obey her. As a child, Kitty had been the playmate of Miss Kate Savage, of Sketrick Castle. They to each other had always borne a striking personal resemblance. The name Kate they shared in common, but the commoner name of Kitty had been adopted by the plebeian child. Even Miss Savage, and her father Philip Savage, had used every effort to induce the old man to change his means of living. The effort of the patrician was like the effort of the plebeian daughter—idle.

There she stood on the gentle seashore shading her eyes from the sunlight, awaiting her father's return.

Presently the boat draws near the shore—near enough to admit of her seeing the occupants distinctly.

Her father is not there; Jamey Gordon sitting at the tiller of her father's boat, and her father not with him! There was something wrong. The wind died away. How slowly they came; oh, how slowly! At last they are within earshot.

"Where's father, Jamey?" she shouted. Jamey did not answer. Had she not called loudly enough?

"Is my father not there?" she cried again.

This time Jamey could not evade the question.

"He's here," he said, pointing to the bows of the boat.

"Is he hurt?"

"Yes."

Gordon took down the sail, and with a few strokes of the oar brought the boat close to the shore.

"How did it happen?" she cried; and the poor girl, wild with excitement for the father she loved so well, ran out into the cold December sea to meet her stricken parent. It was a sad, sad sight. The harvest of blood had commenced.

In a few minutes she knew it all. Her father had been wounded in the side by a blunderbuss discharged by one of the King's men. "At first he thocht it was only a bit scratch, an' managed tae get aff," she was told.

"But by an' bye it turned oot mair."

Such was the tale told by Jamey Gordon. She listened to his breathing. It was thick and low. Yes, there he lay. One glance at the glassy eye told that his hour was fast approaching. The sturdy active fisherman could neither speak nor stir. They carried him tenderly to his cottage. They laid him gently in his own bed. They tended him carefully, and sent for the leech at Killyleagh. The daughter watched him through the long hours. She never left his bedside.

Mr. Cathcart, commonly known as Dr. Corncat, was the only doctor in the neighbourhood, and his practice extended for many miles on every side. He was a jolly little red-faced man, gifted more with worldly discretion than medical knowledge. His treatment consisted for the most part of one or two specifics which he disguised under long names, many of them very ridiculous; most of them very harmless. In surgical cases his treatment was rough, and in the present day would be called cruel. Still, if Dr. Corncat was cruel, it was not intentional. A more good-natured or a better liked man was not known in the district. His jokes were genial and pleasant his laugh ever ready; and. whether he prescribed pounded spiders or vipers' fat, or bled the patient who was dying for want of blood, he was always a welcome visitor until he asked for his fee. Then the broad grin on the mouth of Hodge disappeared at once, and that organ closed like a rattrap. Such was Dr. Corncat, who in the troubled times of 1636 and subsequent years played so important a part in the history of Killyleagh. It was he who, during Phelim O'Neill's rebellion in that year in Ulster, whipped the town bailie with his own hands because he refused to drink to the health of the Merry Hearts of Down. It was he who, during those same troublous times, tied the hands of Tom Hannigan of the Texe to the old pump at Balloo crossroads, when Tom rashly asserted that he did not care a fig for "The Dutchman." But to our story.

The little doctor rode up to the house, his round face glowing with health and the ride in the clear frosty air. The handle of his riding whip was as usual stuck in his mouth, and a black bag of clumsy instruments of torture hung in his hand. As he approached he was met by a fussy old woman usually styled Mother Jellie, whose greatest pride was to make herself useful in cases of sickness or death.

"Ye may e'en gang back hame again, docther," said the lady. "Ye're owre late tae dae ony guid tae Wullie Sinclair."

"Why, mother," said the doctor, "is he worse?"

"Na, he's a heap betther; but if you come near him ye'll be cuttin' an' carvin' at him tae nae purpose but tae pit ye in min' o' yer young days—"

"Hoot, mother, for shame! Tell me how he is?"

"Weel, tae be plain wi' ye, he is deed—deed as a maggot, docther—shot by some o' thae murderers they ca' King's men. Perdition seize them an' the King thegither."

"Are you mad, Mother Jellie, to speak ill o' the King Charles, and the country round in such a state! Come in, mother, come in till I see the poor fellow they have murdered."

It was, indeed, too late. The silver cord was loosed. The pitcher was broken at the well. Only a form of clay reposed beneath a home-made sheet! Only a fisher's daughter mourned beside the bed. It was a sad blow to Kitty. Alone in the house—a girl of eighteen summers! But she had comforters. Neighbours came and gave advice. He had been shot by a King's man at the Bar of Strangford—his only crime consisted in assisting the "Jack o Lantern" over the bar. Foremost among the mourners came Philip Savage and his daughter Kate; not to recapitulate the good deeds of the deceased fisherman, but to console and to devise for the future of Kitty. Theirs was practical comforting.

The day of the funeral came round. Fierce wind, laden with snow, raged over the earth. The fisherman went to his long home in the old green, now robed in white, where slept his forefathers and his dearest friends. Kitty, his daughter, was left alone upon the world in utter, black despair. Good old Mother Jellie, her neighbour, proposed to come and stay with her for a night or two, and her offer was gladly accepted. After the expiration of a few days, it had been arranged that Kitty Sinclair was to go away out into the world. For a short time she was to go to school at Carrickfergus at the sole expense of Philip Savage, of Sketrick. Indeed, this gentleman had frequently pressed on her, at his daughter's solicitation, to go to school during the lifetime of her father; but she had steadfastly refused to do so. Now, when that father was no more, she would go "anywhere, anywhere, out of the world."

So she had at last given her consent. For so far she had grown up only with a little better education than that becoming her station in life, notwithstanding the offers of advancement repeatedly made by the kind-hearted neighbours. The all-engrossing love for her father had thwarted their generous designs. Surely the death of the father was the way taken by Heaven for the advancement of the daughter! So you would say. So said Mother Jollie and the mourners.

On the fourth day after the funeral, when the decencies of wearing apparel could be obtained, she would go to school This was the programme. How true is it in this world that man proposes, but God disposes. It was not no arranged.

# CHAPTER IV

## THE LOVERS—THE FIRST WARNING—A SECRET

It was a bleak, wild winter evening at Sketrick Castle. It was the evening of the day on which Willie Sinclair had been laid to rest in Killinchy Churchyard. The snow without lay thick upon the ground, wrapping all Nature in its ermine mantle, and, borne on the wings of the wild and furious gusts, was beating against the faces of the pedestrians who happened to be abroad giving to the whole scene a bleak and miserable appearance. But of all the bleak places in this bleak world, on this wild, fearful night, Sketrick Castle was the very bleakest. The sea roared and tumbled over the rough stone causeway connecting the Island of Sketrick, on the Killinchy side of Lough Cuan, with the mainland, as if it would thoroughly overthrow that ruinous old fabrick and ever afterwards isolate the castle from the shore. Through the turrets of that venerable mansion—for our readers must not suppose it was then the square tumble-down place it now is—the wind whistled and howled most dismally, and through the long corridors that stood behind the square fortress came sudden gusts that chilled to the bone and cut like a knife. Strange, inexplicable sounds, too, came crashing through those ancient halls that made the strongest tremble, and even the old servants faint with terror. There was a legend of some weird and dreadful ghost connected with almost every room in the old part of the building. Each chamber had been famous for some bloody murder, or some dreadful crime committed long ago, but the particulars of which still lived fresh within the memory of the old residents of Sketrick. Willie Gilmore, the henchman, the fisherman, in fact the man about the castle, was the only one of the domestics who did not share this fear. His forefathers had been connected with the castle for many generations, as his posterity have lived there after him, and Gilmore's Bay is still pointed out to the curious tourist by the quaint old shores of Strangford. Here many remnants of the old Gilmore race reside, preserving to this day the old family name Gilmore far better and far purer than many that the world calls noble.

But the old portion of the building of Sketrick was then very little used by the family of the Savages. There was far more than sufficient accommodation in the newer part of it, and perhaps the mystic dread of the older part had as much to do with keeping it untenanted as anything else. Another reason was that the family of Philip Savage consisted only of one daughter, Kate, the pride of her old father's heart.

All the fury of the elements was thus raging round the venerable mansion on this evening. The servants had huddled from the servants' half for refuge in the kitchen, and to them, half dead with fear, Willie Gilmore was recounting a succession of dreadful stories connected with the several haunted rooms within the castle, and putting the housemaid and Betty Long, the cook, into that delightful state of mind that makes one start and look round at the slightest sound.

But there was none of this feeling in the black oak parlour of Sketrick Castle on this wild and dreary evening. The wind outside might whistle as it pleased, and roar and dash and tear along—the sea might lash the solid walls and foam and boil over "the White Rock," a short distance off – there was little thought of it, I ween, in that cosy room. There sat Kate Savage and young Hugh de Montgomerie of Rosemount, son of

Hugh Montgomery, and commonly called the Earl of Strangford, to whom she was shortly to become united in the holy bonds of matrimony. They were deep in earnest conversation as to the great event of their lives, and with all the sincerity of deep and true affection they sat clasped in each other's arms, and whispered in each other's ears their future prospects and their future vows.

They had been sitting thus for some time, and as the storm without grew louder and louder, the lovers within grew more and more confiding.

"And must you go back before it?" said the fair Kate, as she gazed into the eyes of her lover.

"Yes, my dearest, but three days will soon pass, when we 'shall meet to part no more'—to use the words of that good man Livingstone on the last Sabbath."

"Oh, I do love that good gentlemen!" said Kate, with all the rapture of her age; "the people of Killinchy are surely blessed in having such a pastor!"

"They are blessed, Kate; let us hope he may long be spared to work among them. William Hamilton of Ballybreagh is always with him now since he lost his child."

"That is a change, indeed, and I hope no difficulties may arise to mar this good work. God knows, we hear mutterings enough."

"You must not heed the rumours of the idle people about the rising of the enemies of our religion, my dear."

"But if they should—"

"Do not fear, my love, there are plenty of stout men yet in County Down to put down any attempt at insurrection."

"We will be married before that, at all events, Hugh, dear."

"Yes, love; but do not think of these evil things more."

"You will go to your uncle's at Portaferry to-morrow, dearest?"

"So it is arranged, for my uncle Patrick sent a boat for me last night. Oh, I hope the weather may take up!" and the fair girl clasped her hands devoutly.

"How is that poor girl, Kate, you called on yesterday?"

"Oh, you mean Kitty Sinclair of Ringhaddie. She is even better than could be expected, and the people say we are liker each other than ever."

"Like you, Kate; she must be good, then!"

"Yes, Hugh, the people do say she and I are very like each other. You know we are both about the same age. She has been a good deal with me one way and another. Why, uncle Pat Savage, of Portneferry, once mistook her for me when he met her on the shore. He has always taken a great interest in her, and often wished to give her a better education."

"And did she refuse his offer?"

"Yes, while her father lived; but now since his death she has consented to go to school to Carrickfergus."

"Was not this the girl who was to have been your brides-maid, darling?"

"Yes; but now, you know, that is out of the question."

Thus the lovers talked and prattled, and by and bye their conversation turned on certain matters which were no doubt very interesting to themselves, but of which you and I, gentle reader, have no business to hear more.

As gust after gust of wintry wind swept through the towers of Sketrick, it was evident the nerves of Miss Savage were becoming unstrung. She had passed through a day of wild excitement in connection with the case of her friend Kitty Sinclair. On several occasions, as a blast of more than ordinary fierceness struck the building, it seemed as if she was fainting.

Suddenly, at one of those awful gusts of wind that shook the poor old mansion in its fury, the eyes of Kate Savage changed their expression. First they appeared wild and angry, then a film spread over them, her body stiffened in the arms of her lover, and her head fell heavily on his shoulders. He cried aloud for aid, but in the wild fury of the night his shrieks were answered by unearthly moans and howlings, and vacant, senseless laughter from the old rooms and passages above.

The house was aroused. The fainting form of the girl was carried to her room. For an hour or more the anxious lover paced the room in terrible anxiety. The old nurse every now and then entered and gave him such comfort as she could. At the end of the time named Hugh de Montgomerie was admitted to her chamber. The swoon—that figure of death—had passed away. She lay upon the bed weak and exhausted. As the young man entered the room her colour returned, and the bright love-look beamed from her eyes again.

"Oh, Hugh," she said, "I have had such a fearful dream or vision, and yet so like reality. Pray, love, that it may never be reality, but I fear it is a warning. It was so clear and vivid. I fear it portends death to some of us.

As if it were my last command, I charge you, should anything happen to me, dearest Hugh, to look in my—"

She stopped abruptly. No effort of his could induce her to say more of her dream. If he referred to it, she met the reference with a reproof or a laugh. "*Varium et mutabile semper femina.*"

As Hugh de Montgomery was retiring for the night he met the old nurse on the stairs.

"Oh, sir," said the nurse, "did she tell you the vision?"

"No, but you will confer on me an everlasting debt of gratitude——"

"I cannot tell," she replied. "Miss Savage told me nothing except this."

"What was that?"

"She repeated certain words which she caused me to write

on paper. Then she told me that there was mischief in the air and directed me to retain that paper until after her marriage."

"Will you show me the paper?"

"Here it is, sir, but I can make no meaning out of it;" and she handed him a paper on which the sand from the sandbox still adhered. He took the paper and read these words—

"Keep back, Hugh—oh, take your hand from my throat!— what! a knife!—I tell you that I am another's!"

The writing was a puzzle to him as it had been to the old nurse. Discreetly making a copy of it, he returned the original to the nurse and treasured his copy, with the intention of seeking an explanation when he had a right to demand it. Within one week they would be man and wife. The secret might then he revealed.

The wild wind shrieked around Sketrick, and the stars were hid. Could he have read those stars, fair reader, he would have seen that the week he mentioned would be long and weary waiting.

# CHAPTER V

## ON THE SEA

It is the 6th of December, 16—. The day has been bright, and, for the season, very mild. It is evening. The western sun beams on the Killinchy knolls, lighting up one side and leaving the other in shade. In the distance the massive cone of Slieve Donard throws a shadow over the plain, and the few scattered farm houses are basking in the declining light. The repose of a winter's night is settling over the country.

The "Jack o Lantern" is once more under weigh. Wattie Martin and his trusty crew are wearing the good ship out from the primitive harbour of Killyleagh. There may have been speculation on the part of many of that crew as to whither the "Jack" was bound so soon after the last cruise. But their speculation was kept to themselves. Their confidence in Wattie was too well founded to seek information which they knew would not be given. He had led them long enough through many a scrape to be thoroughly known to his men. They know him to such an extent, and trusted him sufficiently, to know that the "Jack" was moving out in obedience to superior knowledge— knowledge which would be theirs when the proper time came. Wattie stood at the rudder, and the "Jack o Lantern" held along the shore. One by one the familiar islands and headlands on the coast crept into view and faded in the distance. They passed the noble edifice of Sketrick looming like an irregular blotch against the saffron tintings of the sky. Next came Ring-haddie Castle and then the Island of Mahee, with its ancient church and monastery, out of the wintry sea. Onward they passed, still holding on their way until the smack stood in the little bay outside the village of Ardmillan, then composed of only a few fishermen's houses. Here they lay to, and impressive silence fell upon them all. Presently in the darkness a boat shot from the lee of the "Jack o Lantern," and rapidly but silently made for the shore.

An hour or more was spent in idleness. Darkness was upon the face of the waters. The moon was not due till later on, and the season of darkness was taken full advantage of by these hardy adventurers.

By and bye, three whistles sounded over the dark water. Was it the sound of the curlews moving inland front the advancing tide? If so, the cry was answered, from the deck of the little vessel on whose movements we have been playing the spy. Then the splash of oars falling with a regular sweep was heard above the ripple of the water on the bow.

"'Jack' ahoy!" was called in a low and muffled voice.

"Ay, ay!"

The boat stopped alongside the "Jack." Several figures crept over the side. One of them carried a burden, with which he proceeded straightway to the cabin, which had been specially rigged up and appropriated for the reception of a fair but unwilling voyager. Then the boat was hauled up to the davits and placed on board. The anchor was tripped. The great wings of the "Jack" were rapidly spread, the helm put down, and the freshening breeze caught up the gentle craft and drove it onward towards the sea.

The cabin of the smack contained two berths, or bunks, as they were more familiarly called. These sleeping places were as uncomfortable as could well be conceived. At the head of each bunk was a small recess on which a door was placed. In this recess the occupant of the berth placed any article of value. One of these places was occupied by Wattie; the other by Steenie Gilmore, his mate. However, the cabin had been done up as daintily as rough hands could arrange it, and given over wholly to the occupation of the lady who had come on board. How she liked the apartment or relished their homely attentions they had no opportunity of knowing. She remained below as if she had been a close prisoner.

The bright full moon peeped boldly from behind Ballywhite mountain, and showed a glittering track of silver wavelets inviting the little ship to follow.

Presently a muffled figure came aft and entered into conversation with Wattie. A glimpse at his features, favoured by the moon, showed that he was the stranger who had chartered the "Jack" at Killyleagh.

"Well Wattie, I'm glad to say that I have been successful, and I trust that the swift heels of your little vessel will do the rest."

"A'm richt gled, sir," said Wattie, "that ye hae been fortunate, and hope yer sister'll no be ony the waur o' her sail in sich a puir place as the cabin o' the 'Jack.'"

"Oh, it's very good. Wattie," replied the stranger. "At first she was very unwilling to accompany me, but after a little persuasion she agreed. Then again, with the usual uncertainty of a woman's movements, she regretted that she had given her consent, and would have struggled to return—"

"You dinna mean tae say she changed her mind, sir?"

"Ay did she, lad, and got so outrageous that I do believe she would have succeeded in making her escape—for I would scorn to use force, you know—but that her violence brought its own punishment."

"What dae ye mean, sir?"

She swooned, and in a fiat of unconsciousness I carried her on board. What place is that?"

"That's Kirkcubben, sir, and yonner whaur ye see the spot

26

o' lan' comin' oot intil the sea is the best place for a shot at the barnacles and widgeons aboot a' this airt."

Thus conversing, they beguiled the time while the "Jack" shot past Ballyhendry, Portneferry, and finally out into the open sea. Then the held was put about and they stood for the North Coast of France.

. . . . .

Two nights after the "Jack o Lantern" was anchored in the bay of St. Malo, then one of the most important places of trading for men of Wattie's class. At midnight the boat was launched. The stranger, accompanied by the muffled figure of a woman, took their places, and in a few minutes the regular sound of retreating oars was once more heard above the rippling of the waves.

When the men returned who had manned the boat, Wattie summoned the crew together. On the table of the empty cabin he placed a little heap of the golden guineas which he had received from the stranger. Then dividing it proportionately over his men, he made arrangements for obtaining a good supply of contraband liquor for his return. But as the smuggling part of Wattie's business is the one with which we have least business, we need not dwell any longer on that which least concerns us.

Little did Wattie think of the importance of his last adventure. He could not have surmised—he could not have believed the awful consequences of his voyage, nor how much he had contributed to the sad events that were at this moment racking so many quiet homes. Even now, after the absence of so many years, the effects of Wattie's voyage are still felt. He contributed, without knowing to what extent, to an event which has remained for nearly three hundred years a mystery. But we must not await Wattie's return. With the speed of fancy we fly across the channel, and resume our truthful narrative on the shores of Lough Cuan. Events there have been following each other in rapid succession. The wail of the orphan has been heard over the country. And now the tears of the gentle must mingle with the tears of the simple. Hardship, misfortune, and trouble are not confined to any creed nor peculiar to any class.

# CHAPTER VI

## HASTE TO THE WEDDING—
## THE DREAM IS REALISED—
## MYSTERY

The day was approaching for the celebration of the marriage. Hugh de Montgomerie, of Rosemount, son of Hugh de Montgomerie, of Rosemount, Esquire, and Kate Savage of Sketrick, daughter of Philip Savage, of Sketrick and Mahee, and niece of Patrick Savage, of Portneferry, Esquire, were to be wedded on the following day. The old castle of Ringhaddie was the destined home of the happy pair, for the bride wished to remain near her father in his declining years. The bride elect had been spending the last two days with her uncle at Portneferry, preparing, with the assistance of her aunt and cousins, the necessaries for the change in her life.

Kate Savage left Portneferry on the 6th December, two days before the day appointed for the wedding, and she and Hugh were to meet that evening at her father's residence at Sketrick. As the storm still continued, and she was fearful on account of the dream which we have related in the previous chapter, to come by boat, she started in her father's coach to proceed by the road skirting the northern and western shores of the romantic lough. Her only companion was Tom Munn, the coachman, an old dependant of her father. Her cousins, it was arranged, were to come over in the boat on the following day to assist the wedding ceremony, which was to take place on the 8th December.

29

# THE MYSTERY OF STRANGFORD LOUGH

On the way home she found that the news of the approaching nuptials had spread far and wide through the Ards. As the cavalcade moved onward they stopped for a few minutes at the ruins of the Old Abbey, which had been destroyed by fire about thirty years previously by Sir Brian Mac-Felim O'Neill, lest it might be converted into a garrison for the English troops. The road past the ruins had been strewn with fresh oaten straw, interspersed with green boughs. Here her father-in-law caught her in his arms and kissed her. Then the crowd sent up a ringing cheer that was returned by a vast assemblage on Ballyboley hill, on which several bonfires had been lighted.

Then old Hugh Taylor, of Blackabbey, who for many a year had been ploughman to the family, came forward and caught the damsel in his arms, and actually kissed her before anyone expected. The girl herself was at first surprised; but, on looking at the venerable old man, and hearing the plaudits of the crowd, she sensibly gave him one of her sweetest smiles, and passed forward on her wedding march.

At Newtown, too, or, as it was sometimes called, Ballyno, there was general rejoicing. Flags floated from the high turret of the great castle, and the big bell in the church, dedicated to St. Columba, or Columbkille, welled out as merry a note as every casting rang. The crowd in Greenwell Street was immense. Here old Tom Wallace, the piper, met the party, and insisted on performing his merriest tune in front of the coach. No man was more popular than Hugh de Montgomerie, of these old days. Bonfires blazed on Scrabo, and another cheer sent her on her way to Comber, then vulgarly called "Cummer," where another ovation of a somewhat similar character awaited her.

The marriage was to take place on the 8th of December, in the meeting-house of Killinchy, and after partaking of the dinner, to be provided by the bride's father, in Sketrick Castle, the young couple were to depart for Downpatrick, and thence for Dublin, before taking up their abode in the Castle of Ring-haddie. Such was the programme. We shall see how far Fate furthered their desires.

On the 6th December the young Earl arrived at Sketrick Castle with the lawyer and the settlement. He was filled with the most glorious anticipations of happiness, but found that his fair Kate had not as yet reached home. It was not often she was behindhand in her trysts since the early days of courtship, in which it is, we believe, unusual for young ladies to weary out their lovers, and impose taxes upon their patience.

The bridegroom elect, with impatient longing, kept waiting for the arrival of his betrothed until the bright hues of the morning faded into twilight. Sometimes he would wander round the coast viewing her dearly loved islands of Sketrick, Rainish, and Mahee, and watch, with pensive longing, the fishermen spreading their nets upon the beach, or the wild sea-bird screaming as it flew far inland. Sometimes he would wander up to the top of Killenikin Knowehead to the seat on which he had often sat with his own Kate, and gaze on the hundred islands at his feet, or cast his eyes down towards Ardmillan, in vain looking for the approach of his mistress. Thus did the young lover strive to pass the hours till the long shadows lengthened and went out, enveloping the little world around in one determined shadow, and with this shadow fell a shadow on his heart—a sense of ill he could not well withstand—a deep and awful omen of events he dreaded, yet could not name.

Inside the castle all was confusion and turmoil; for everyone was busy making preparations for the coming event. Old Philip Savage wandered through the house endeavouring to hasten on the work, but in reality keeping it back. The only person in the house who was thoroughly in her glory was old

Betty Long, the cook. Now she had an opportunity of displaying her marvellous skill—a skill of which she often boasted, and even wept for an opportunity of exhibiting. "It was the guid auld days comin' back to Sketrick," she said, "when cooks was cooks."

Meanwhile deeper and deeper grew the shadows round the castle; higher and wilder rose the mournful wind, making the windows rattle and the old rooms shriek; ghastly, and more ghastly swelled the wild, unearthly wailings from the haunted chambers of the mansion. And yet no Kate. Her lover by this time was in a fearful state of excitement, but endeavoured to allay his agitation by assisting her father to rearrange the library for the twentieth time at least.

Suddenly there is a cry—"Here is Miss Kate!" and the old coach came rumbling over the causeway which connects the island with the shore, and the cold grey moon sent slanting down its beams, lending a lustre, in the lover's eyes, to that battered old coach. At a glance it was perfectly apparent that Tom Munn, the coachman, was drunk. The reins were hanging loosely in his hand. He was busy mumbling to himself some wild old song, as the jaded horses drew up at the door, evidently more through their own natural sagacity than by his guidance. But who cares or cared for Tom Munn, the coachman? On such an occasion the marriage of his master's daughter it was lawful to get drunk, and the young lover darted past him and opened the coach door.

"Here's the purty bride!" said Tom Munn, as he pulled the horses on their haunches in front of the castle. Then the old man commenced to sing—

> "She's a right girl;
> Fol de diddle di do."

"Kate, my love!" said Hugh de Montgomerie, "we thought you would never be here," as he peeped into the coach.

"Thocht she wad never be here, an' Tam Munn drivin'! Ah, well, A maun thole, A maun thole!" and the man of endurance sang again.

But not a word responsive came from the interior of the coach. By the reflection of the pale moonlight the figure of Miss Savage was seen sitting, or rather lying, in the far corner, mute and motionless, and the old man on the box kept mumbling forth his song.

"Kate, are you ill or sleeping?" said the lover, and stretched forth his hand, and took hers within his own. It was cold and damp. A deadly paleness seized him, and he almost fell swooning on the ground. Then all was silent – silent, save for the lethargic singing of the coachman, and a constant drip, drip, drip, that struck dread terror to the hearts of all who heard it.

"A light, a light!" shouted Philip Savage, as he supported the youth now recovering from the shock he had received at the cold touch of her hand.

"Li' my pipe, an' let's have 'nether glass!" bawled the coachman, in his drunkenness.

A light was brought; the young man grasped it eagerly and looked into the coach and over his shoulder hung the father of the bride, pale, anxious, and haggard. The fair girl was sitting in the corner, her head sunk upon her breast in sleep. In sleep—aye, so you would have said, but that on her cloak and on her dress there was a stream of dark and clotted gore. Her feet were resting in a pool of blood, from which the light of the torch was fearfully reflected; and still there came that drip, drip, drip, all solemn, slow, and constant.

"Kate! my God, what is this?" shouted father and lover in one breath, and then they bent within the coach and tried to wake the sleeper, but in vain. Her husband that was to be laid his hand upon her brow, cold and clammy to the touch, and gently raised the head and parted the long flaxen curls that used to lie so lovingly on his shoulder. What a sight then met the eyes of both! A long gash from ear to ear had almost severed head from trunk, and the sweet, gentle face was hacked and disfigured. Her head falling down over her breast had kept the wound together, and in a great measure presented the flow of blood; but now when the head was raised it fell loosely against the back of the coach, and the crimson river spouted forth afresh, the heart blood of the bride dyeing the hand of the bridegroom.

She slept. Yes, within that old baronial coach she slept the sleep of death, and the coachman on the box kept singing to himself all the time this shocking scene was being enacted, for there was no one to bid him be still. She slept, and beside her stood her lover—husband almost—and the fond father of her early days. She slept, and the cold grey moon kept shining on the scene, and the wild wind kept howling on, and the shrill wailing came round the castle turrets. The bride of Sketrick slept. It was then those terrible words of hers recurred to the memory of the young Earl—the ominous words she had used in the swoon. It was then he first began to see some reality in the mysterious prophecy, of which only part as yet had come true. Those muttered words came back to his recollection with terrible distinctness:

"Keep back, sir—oh, take your hand from my throat!— what! a knife!—I tell you that I am another's."

Thus thinking, the strong man bent his head upon his breast and tenderly carried the mangled remains into the castle.

# CHAPTER VII

## MORE TROUBLE IN
## KILLINCHY

Again the grave opened to receive its dead. With solemn and measured tread a large concourse of people filed over the hill of Killinchy. In front of them an oaken coffin is borne by four sturdy tenants of Mr. Savage. Beside the stricken father, immediately behind the coffin, walks Livingstone, the pastor of Killinchy, whose reverend figure was followed by the gaze of a loving flock‡. Beside them walked the young Earl (as Hugh Montgomerie was commonly styled), accompanied by a young man with whom he had made acquaintance, and between whom there shortly sprang up a tender bond of sympathy. This young man was Samuel Stewart, of Sketrick, a man of good appearance, sound discretion, and strong will; a man who afterwards became the progenitor of a long line of descendants. The circumstances of the death had become public, and this fact, coupled with the indignation of the country at the foul assassination, led to the assemblage of an immense number of people. From Ardmillan, Tullycore, Ballydorn, and along the whole shore to Killyleagh there were representatives from all the families.

---

‡ Rev. John Livingstone (1603-1672) from Stirlingshire was the first Presbyterian Minister of Killinchy from 1630 until 1634 when he was deposed and fled in the *'Eagle Wing'* in 1636 with other 'non-conforming' dissenting ministers including Rev. Robert Blair of Bangor Abbey.

# THE MYSTERY OF STRANGFORD LOUGH

And now the mournful procession has entered the precincts of the graveyard and the great band of staunch Presbyterians unite in singing the strains of the 23rd Psalm as they reverently approach the open grave. Here Livingstone addressed them with the eloquence which has made his name revered in this portion of the country, and with Presbyterian simplicity and solemnity the coffin is left in its last resting-place. The crowd quietly and sadly dispersed, and the old man walked forth childless. It was a heavy blow both to him and to Montgomerie.

As the old man left the graveyard leaning on his friend and pastor, he observed a commotion in the crowd before him. It was evident something was the matter concerning Philip Savage, but it was plain from the motions of the people that they wished to prevent him being annoyed at this season.

"There is something wrong among my people. If you will permit me I will inquire the cause," said Livingstone as he drew his arm from Savage's, and moved forwards towards an excited group. But before he had reached them, a woman rushed wildly out from the crowd towards the pastor.

"Oh, minister, dear," she said excitedly, "this is a black day for Killinchy. The bonnie lassie that went to skule has no' been heard o' syne she left."

"What do you mean, Sally?" he asked.

"What dae A mean or wha shud A mean but Kitty Sinclair. She haesna been heard tell o' since she left tae gang tae Carrick."

"How did you hear this news, Sally?" asked the clergyman with an affection of unbelief.

"It was my ain son, yer reverence, that drove her on the wy tae Cumer. An' just as they come by the ghaist hole—ye ken the ghaist hole, yer reverence—he observed a muckle bright licht fleein' up an' doon ower the watter. But gude save us—

beggin' yer pardin fur the word, sir—but ye maun see till Mr. Savage."

The quick wit of the woman had observed the change on the features of the old man, who had joined Livingstone in time to hear her last words. The news of the disappearance of Kitty following so closely upon the murder of his own daughter was too much for the old frame, already broken with the weight of years. He clasped Livingstone's convulsively, and fell in a swoon into the arms of Samuel Stewart, who caught him in time to prevent his falling upon the ground. The crowd of onlookers increased. With their native curiosity they thronged round the prostrate figure of the old man. Speculation became general. Savage was at length aroused and placed in his carriage, and by the assistance of his friends he was removed to Sketrick Castle—older by twenty years than he had been barely one week previously.

The blow was a severe one not alone to Philip Savage. Hugh de Montgomerie felt it acutely. Nay, they all in and around the castle experienced the sad feelings death is wont to impale when one we love has been suddenly removed. The great respect in which the old man was held by the whole countryside made the visitation more impressive. The farmers and yeomen, the fishermen and peasants, banded themselves together as detectives and strove to discover the perpetrator of the deed. They patrolled the roads in the neighbourhood; they sat up at night, examined all the fishing boats upon the lough or upon the islands; they retraced the steps of the carriage in which Miss Savage had driven from Portneferry, and they searched for some definite clue as to the disappearance of Kitty Sinclair. But the search ended where it began. Sally Ritchie's drunken son could tell little more than he had already told his mother, and he mixed up his story so wonderfully on cross-examination that the people placed little or no reliance on his tale.

To one person he ascribed her disappearance to supernatural agency, and gave a remarkably accurate description of one of the ghosts that are said to dwell in the arm of the sea called the "ghost-hole," near Comber. To another he told how at least a dozen men had pounced upon him, while another dozen at the least had seized Kitty, and tying her hands and feet, had drowned her in that hole which bore so horrible a reputation.

No clue could be found; it became a nine days' wonder. As such around the country it soon ceased to attract much attention. The short, dark winter days grew gradually longer. A deeper and warmer tint crept slowly over the sky, and the candles and rushlights lasted longer by reason of the shorter nights. But round the pleasant bays of Sketrick, or the hilly roads of Killinchy, the fair forms of Miss Savage and Kitty Sinclair were seen no more, for the one slept in the churchyard and the other had not been found. The farmers and the yeomen; the fishermen and the peasants, gave up their search. The mystery of their disappearance was the Mystery of Strangford Lough.

# CHAPTER VIII

## THE UNWINDING OF THE SKEIN

Three months have elapsed since the events occurred which have been related in the previous chapters. The months hung heavily on the hands of the young Earl. Indeed, it was a sad time to almost all the persons who have been introduced to the reader's attention. For a long time his friends feared for the reason of Hugh de Montgomerie. He was in the habit of wandering through the country in an aimless idiotic manner. At one time he would saunter for hours about the knowehead of Killenikin, and again he would roam about the green vales and sunny slopes of Killinchy. By the whole neighbourhood he was beloved and respected. The kindly hearts of the Killinchy people sympathised with him in his trouble. Often times, accompanied by Livingstone, the first Presbyterian preacher in this district, he would wander through the quiet churchyard; or accompany that reverend pastor in his visitations. Often times alone he would sit for hours by the silent grave, courting a moody and useless melancholy. On other days he spent much of his time at the house of a man named Stewart, of Sketrick, who had one son, a young man about the same age as Montgomerie, and between these two, although occupying different spheres in life, a sincere attachment sprang up.

Notwithstanding his quiet and resigned demeanour, a new passion had taken possession of the young Earl—the passion for revenge. He did not breathe it to Livingstone, but Stewart soon discovered his feelings, and strove to turn them to account. He proposed to him to go abroad to search for the murderer. Not with any hope of discovering the perpetrator of the crime so much as to try a change of scene to divert the mind of his friend from its gloomy forebodings.

At the time of which we resume our narrative the mystery of the murder the disappearance of Kitty Sinclair had ceased to occupy that prominence in the public mind which it had occupied for so long a time. There were no newspapers to keep it alive by publishing details. The wonder and the talk had remained paramount for more than nine days, but the time had arrived when it maintained a less prominent hold upon the public mind and the public conversation.

It is true that the myrmidons of the law had exerted themselves to discover the guilty parties, and had ended where they had begun. They had absolutely discovered nothing. The lover, if he wished to find the clue to the crimes, must find it for himself. He was content to take up the matter where they left it.

It was at last arranged that he should leave the country for the benefit of his health, and young Stewart was to accompany him in his wanderings. They had no settled plan—nothing was definite. Ostensibly the journey was undertaken for the sake of health; really to roam recklessly over the world at large in the hope of making some discoveries. Two facts alone were prominent. The first was that Kate Savage had been murdered between the town of Comer and Sketrick Castle on the evening of the 6th December. The second, that Kitty Sinclair had left Ringhaddie on the same day, and had not since been heard of. The two events seemed linked together; and if so, there were more persons than one mixed up in the crimes.

By a strange reticence where such silence was almost culpable, the Earl did not confide to Stewart the dream or trance in which his dearly beloved one had made use of those singular expressions. Over this he brooded in silence. The copy of the strange words which he had obtained from the nurse on the night of the fainting fit he kept concealed about his own person.

Latterly the companionship between Montgomerie and Stewart had been such that the latter frequently stayed all night in the castle. On the night on which the events occurred to which we now draw attention he occupied the same room which he had been accustomed to use on the occasions of his remaining overnight.

The room to which Stewart retired for the night was one already familiar to our readers. It was a small apartment in the square turret, the remains of which still grace with their ruined beauty the western side of the Island of Sketrick. The entrance to the room was by a door leading from the lobby. Another door led from this bedroom into a storeroom or dressing-room. A bright fire blazed upon the hearth, and glinting flames threw the furniture of the room into bold relief. The bed was placed nearly opposite the fire, and at its head to the right wall was a small embrasured window in the thick wall. The furniture consisted of the usual homely articles in constant use at the time. It had been Miss Savage's own room, and it still bore traces of her care. It was the room into which she had been carried on the night which she had been seized with the swoon. Over the mantelpiece there hung a sampler wrought by herself, a remembrancer of her schooldays. The only other mural decorations consisted of a picture of her mother and an oil painting of some remote ancestor of the Savages. The bed was a massive affair, such as was only to be seen in the homes of the more wealthy; and the only other articles of furniture to which there is any occasion to draw the attention of the reader were the armchair in which he sat, and an old bureau made of black. It had been given as a present to Miss Savage from her uncle in Portneferry, and was made from the black or bog oak, commonly found in the bogs of Ireland.

On his entering the room Stewart locked both the door by which be entered the apartment and the door leading into the dressing-room. He sat for some time at the fireside pondering over the matters on which he had been conversing with the Earl, and by degrees fell into that reverie which a blazing fire often induces. After some time he retired to rest, and, as sleep was not pressing him, he lay watching the flickering shadows make strange forms upon the ceiling of his chamber. The moon shone clear and cold upon the fretted pane, and the rays darting through the ivy leaves that surrounded the window produced a mottled shadow on the floor.

He had lain in this way for some time. Whether he had slept or not he was never aware. Suddenly he became conscious of someone in the apartment. He heard no sound of footfall, nor rustling of clothing. He saw nothing, yet he felt the presence. Was it reality, or was it a weird and solemn fancy from which he could not free himself! He was a strong, bold man. Even in those superstitious days he could have laughed you to scorn if you had even suggested the possibility of a ghost. That is to say, if you had made the suggestion in broad daylight. Yet there he lay, frightened at heart without being able to understand the cause of his terror. The fire burned with a sullen glow, but occasionally shot a blaze of light. The wan moon streamed fairly in, pale and clear. A cold perspiration broke over him. He was oppressed by the dread stillness, frightened by the ghostly presence. At last, conquering his nervous fear, he raised himself on his elbow in the bed. The movement made the old bed creak. The fire slipped down, and a momentary blaze threw the objects in the room directly under his view. He looked towards the fire and he saw as it were a misty form seated in the very armchair he had occupied before he retired to rest. "It is fancy," he thought, and rubbed his eyes that he might fathom the supernatural by natural means. When he looked again, the mist had assumed the form of a female figure, seated in the chair. He saw it plainly enough now in outline, for there was no corporeal consistency. It was the figure of a woman, dressed in a grey mantle. Her long hair hung down her back in luxuriant tresses. Slowly the image became more definite, and the face of the woman turned full upon him. That face was white and bloodless. The eyes shone with terrible lustre, and gazed directly into his. As he looked he saw a peculiar mark upon her graceful neck. It became more distinct—like a red ribbon. The occasional gleams of firelight enabled him to see the mark which he had taken for a ribbon was a long ghastly wound extending across the throat!!

It was a desperate hour—a fearful vision! Bold as he was, he trembled like a child, and would have cried out, but that some spell seemed to hold him silent.

Slowly and deliberately the figure arose from the chair, keeping its eyes fixed on him with a long penetrating gaze. Slowly and deliberately it pointed towards the old black bureau. The motion was distinct and intentional. Again he tried to speak, but the mystic figure raised its hand and thus silently forbade him. Was it fact or was it fancy? He observed that the hand raised contained only three fingers! Then the figure melted into mist, and the mist disappeared from the room as quietly and gradually as it had come.

Sam Stewart fell back on his bed exhausted. His nervous system had been too lightly braced. When he opened his eyes the cold grey dawn was breaking over the waters of the lough.

# CHAPTER IX

## WHAT CAME OUT OF THE BUREAU

Samuel Stewart, of Sketrick, was of a genial disposition. Having been of a delicate constitution in infancy, his father had determined that his weakly son should embrace some of the learned professions. With that object in view he had given the youth an education much superior to what might have been expected from his position in life. He had also seen much of the world, for in order to advance his own study he had been obliged to act as tutor to several families not only in London but on the Continent. The hard work had, however, exhausted him; and he was spending a few months at home as an invalid about the time when the events narrated in our earlier chapters were taking place. This education made him less sensitive to superstition. By it he was less likely to look to the supernatural as an explanation for a phenomenon, the cause of which was unknown to him. Still, when he came to think of it next day, try as he would, he found it impossible to account for the vision or appearance of Kate Savage. The figure seated on the chair in the moonlight was the figure of that lady. The remarkable wound on the throat like a red ribbon coincided with the horrible spectacle he had seen three months ago. There, however, the similarity ended. He had observed that the figure held up three fingers only on the right hand, and he was positive that Miss Savage's hand had not been so mutilated. His conversation on the evening before had certainly been of this lady, and if his mind had been excited, it was not un-natural that he should have a lively repetition of the thoughts during the night. But this was too real for a dream. He rec-ollected rubbing his hands and feeling awake. Besides, what did she mean by pointing to the old bureau that stood in the corner of the room? Yes, that might afford a clue. But would it be right for him to open this antique article of furniture without acquainting some of the members of the household? And if he did solicit their assistance and tell them of his dream or spectre—bah! He made up his mind never to speak of the vision, never to think of it more. With this determination he sprang out of bed and proceeded with his toilet.

But the more fixed his determination to forget the lady, the more obtrusive grew that black bureau. He knocked his toe against it as he moved across the floor. One way or another the bureau appeared determined to force itself upon him. Striving to forget or ignore was no use!

Turning to the ancient article of furniture he observed that it was just such a receptacle as that in which one would nat-urally secrete anything of importance. Doubtless it contained many a secret drawer. He sought for a concealed spring or oth-er means of opening the chest. After an hour spent fruitlessly, he was about to abandon the search. At last he discovered by pressing a brass nail that a small panel was shot out of its place. Following up the advantage gained, he was rewarded by find-ing a series of concealed drawers. He tried the drawers, one after the other, but found nothing in any of them which he considered had the slightest reference to the object he had in view. One more drawer was to be tried. He opened it careless-ly. It contained two packets of old letters. The first packet con-tained a number of letters in the handwriting of his friend the Earl of Strangford. They were the love-letters of her affianced suitor, carefully treasured by Miss Savage in the secret recesses of her chamber. Poor Stewart felt he was exhuming a sad relic. The second packet contained a number of letters, of which the covering of only two had been opened. The others were in the same condition as if they only had left the hand of the sender. They were bound round with cord, and on the parcel she had written this curious superscription:

> Not to be shown
> To Hugh till
> I am doubly dead.

"Good, Kate!" said Stewart; "blessed spirit, I shall be the custodian of thy packet. Perhaps these letters will assist us in tracing thy murderers, and but doubly dead, there is a hidden meaning here when she wrote these words—"

The old nurse summoned him to the hall. The substantial breakfast was prepared after the manner of those days. Lord and retainer sat at the same board, and partook of the viands then usually seen on the table of the wealthy.

He concealed the packet of letters in his bosom and replaced the secret drawer of the bureau. In a few minutes they were partaking of that meal which with us would be considered a substantial dinner.

The day was spent by the Earl and Stewart in making preparations for their departure. During the intervals of more active work, Stewart had many serious debates in his own mind as to the meaning of Kate Savage's mystic superscription. Should he show the letters to his friend? This was to him a most perplexing question. If he returned his own love-letters to the Earl, he must account for their production, and perhaps break the injunction as to the others. He came to the conclusion to give the letters to the writer, and to be guided by circumstances as to what he should do next. He was not responsible for the ambiguous nature of the lady's instructions. He did what many another man has done before and since. When unable to decide a serious question for himself he left the decision of that serious question to awkward CHANCE or foolish indecision.

On that evening they bade a tender farewell to the frail old man who had so suddenly lost his daughter. They left old Sketrick Castle, with its once hallowed walks and caves, its bright terrace and sunny aspect. Away into the wide, wide world they went to search for the murderer of the innocent young girl. Without one clue that they knew of, without one definite idea, they started on a path of adventure. Anything, anything for motion. The mystery and sadness of Sketrick was greater than they could bear.

# CHAPTER X

## ON THE TRACK

The evening was bright and warm. The spring had shown symptoms of being unusually early, as our two friends, the Earl of Strangford and Samuel Stewart left the sequestered shores of Killyleagh in the Jack o Lantern. Wattie Martin and his crew were as lively as when we saw them last, and with three lusty cheers from the idlers on the shore the Jack tripped her anchor and sailed from her berth.

"Weel, my lord," said Wattie, as the young Earl stepped on board from the punt which had brought him from the shore, "A'm richt gled to see ye on board o' the auld Jack yince again. Mony an' mony a time has we twa sailed thegither owre the bonny waters of Loch Cowan, when ye wurnae half the size ye ir noo."

"Ay, Wattie, those were happy days. I almost think them coming back, when I feel these old planks beneath my feet. But how's trade, Wattie? Ye'll be getting a rich man, and, I warrant, thriving nobly!"

"Deed an' I daurna compleen, yer honour. Fortune disnae often smile long on us puir fishin' bodies. There's a while o' fillin' an' a while o' fastin' wi' the maist o' us. Auch an' this was sad news aboot Miss Savage!" and the poor fellow, in his love for the daughter of one of the most popular men of the time, almost wept.

"Ay, Wattie, it's a sad blow indeed to more than her father—we all feel it."

"The hale kintra side is just greetin' aboot her. Frae Ballydorn tae Ballyquinton there wusnae a dry e'e amang the

48

dochters of the shore, the cursed day when the news cam' that the bonny girl was murdered. A think the de'il maun hae brauken the chains o' the ither warl', yer honnour, tae dae mischief. A aye blamed mysel' for having onything tae dae wi' carryin' yon couple in the Jack."

Samuel Stewart heard the observations of the sailor, but said nothing then. He feared to say anything to keep alive these sad thoughts in the mind of his companion and friend. On the first opportunity, however, he applied to Wattie for more information.

"What did you mean, Wattie," he said, "by telling the Earl of carrying some persons in your boat."

"What did A mean, Master Stewart? In the ordinar' way, A wudnae hae tell't ony yin o' the rins we hae made, but mony a time A had an inklin' that yon black-avised fellow an' his sister wuz nae guid."

"What blackavised fellow?"

"A fellow wi' three fingers on his richt han'—What ails ye, Master Stewart? Is there ocht wrang?"

"Three fingers on his right hand!"

The action of the figure in his bedroom recurred to his memory. "She held up three fingers," he thought aloud, "and vanished. Are we now on the track?"

As the recollection of that night came back to him, he naturally felt in his pocket for the sealed packet. Yes, it was all right. To prevent any mistake, he descended to the cabin, and, opening the little press at the head of his bunk, he laid the sealed packet carefully in the corner. He then placed beside it some other small articles of his own which he did not wish to carry with him. He had the proofs ready if ever he should be called upon to vouch for the truth of his strange story. Feeling satisfied on this head, he returned to the deck to resume his conversation with Wattie.

49

"You say you had carried over some three-fingered fellow, Wattie; do you know who he was?"

"Nay, sir, I niver heered his name."

"Who was with him?"

"Deed, sir, if I can rightly tell ye. She wuz a woman that he aye ca'ed his sister."

"Why did you not detain them?"

"Why shud A stap them? The young man paid me weel fur drappin' them at St. Malo, an' A min' weel we had a guid run hame."

"Tell me all about it, Wattie," said Stewart; "but, hush! another time. Don't let the Earl hear one word of this."

When a more favourable opportunity offered itself the smuggler told his tale. His narrative ended thus—

"She was aye sayin' when she got the chance that she wusnae his sister ava; but then ye ken he tauld us she was mad wi' love, or somethin', and would say wonderfu' things. But the puir girl didnae get much chance tae talk muckle, bein' kep' sae lang in disguise an' crooned doon in the cabin o' the Jack."

"And you left him where?"

"Deed, an' we jist sent them baith ashore at St. Malo, yer honnour, an' brocht hame as guid a cargo o' auld rum as ever crossed the bar."

"Indeed I fear, Wattie," said Stewart, "that you have done a bad job. However, not one word of this to the Earl. You and I can look about us. If we find anything we can communicate it to him. I would like very much you would run us into St. Malo again. We may not be too late to make some discoveries."

From that moment their destiny was St. Malo—their common object the unravelling of the Mystery of Strangford Lough. They stayed that night at Portneferry, where the crew were sumptuously entertained by Patrick Savage, of that town.

# THE MYSTERY OF STRANGFORD LOUGH

At the conclusion of the entertainment, that gentleman having ordered the boat to be made secure, called all hands of the Jack o Lantern to meet him at the gate of his demesne. Having met them, he conducted them inland to an open spot a short distance from the gate, where a natural hollow existed in the ground. Placing them in this hollow, he addressed the crew as follows:

"My brave Jacks. I have heard from your captain the best accounts of your valour and daring. A better sailor than Wattie Martin, or a braver heart, never sailed over the waters of Loch Cowan. In the distress that rends the hearts of my brother Philip, of Sketrick, and this young man, he has promised to give his utmost aid. I have called you to ask will you join him. Two girls have been plucked from the bosom of our own loved County Down. One has been laid low by a cruel murder, the other has wholly disappeared. There is reason to believe that the same hand committed both these crimes. Will you go to discover the guilty, under the guidance of your captain and these gentlemen? If a reward is wanted I will give one. To each of you, if you bring home either the victim or the villain, it shall be worth more than your share in ten successful runs past the old castle of Strangford; and, on this very spot where you stand I shall give a feast to all who like to come: and every lady who comes to it shall signify her joy of your safe and happy return by allowing herself to be kissed by any man who asks her. Men of Cowan, have I spoken enough? Will you go to rescue the stolen girl, and take vengeance on the murderer?

"We will, we will," started from every throat, till the old woods around re-echoed to their cry. Never did cheers so lusty ring through the woods of Portneferry as the trusty sailors shouted out their pledge of love and reverence.

Early the next morning the Jack o Lantern was under weigh. The shores on both sides of the river were lined with cheering

51

crowds, and when evening came the brave old boat was many a mile from land.

Three days afterwards a little smack entered the harbour of St. Malo, and as soon as all was snug the crew of the Jack o Lantern—for it was our old friend—scattered through the town and port to fish out, if possible, some tidings of the missing pair.

Up to this time Stewart had not divulged to his friend the Earl any of the events connected with his mysterious dream. His silence was maintained for the best reasons. The sealed packet was a sealed packet yet. He feared to produce over-excitement in the mind of Montgomery.

They visited the taverns, the shops, the gens d'armerie, and the prisons. They invited the confidences of garrulous jailers, and were compelled to listen to many strange histories. On these occasions Stewart and Wattie generally contrived to go alone. It would have been imprudent to take the Earl into these places to rend his mind with fruitless questionings. On one of these excursions they had the following conversations with an old jailer of the prison:—

"There had been an execution about a fortnight ago," said the jailer, "and the wretched man had, before he was tied under the fatal guillotine, written a confession of his crimes. Some confess," continued he, "without the torture, and some don't. This one confessed in English, and wrote his confession, and gave it to the governor of the jail. The good magistrates thought he should also confess in French, and tortured him on the rack till he was almost torn asunder. He was a bad boy that Englishman. He murdered an old gentleman in the Place de la Viserieorde and stole 7000 francs."

"And what was the appearance of this scoundrel?" said Stewart, questioning the jailer, more with the desire of humouring him than with the hope of obtaining any information.

"A well-looking man enough, monsieur, but terribly hardened. He had as dark a looking face as anyone would like to see, and by some accident or work of villainy, no doubt, he had lost one of the fingers of his right hand."

"The vera man, the vera man," said Wattie, on this description being interpreted to him. "I noticed them three fingers the first day I gripped his han'. Learn more about him, yer honnour; for I'll wager my life ye hae the rascal noo!"

"Is there no record of his appearance kept by the authorities of your town?"

"Yes, you can have the description I dare say from the Marechal," said the jailer, "who will be glad to let you see his confession, if you can read it."

"Is it in English?"

"Ay, so they say; but many persons who say they can read English have been unable to understand it."

"Did you hear any word of a woman having been in his company?" asked Stewart, straggling to keep down his emotion, as he asked the question.

"A woman—no."

"Not even when the rack was tearing him to pieces?"

"Well, you see, he might have said plenty about women, or anything else he liked, but he spoke in a language none of us understood. It was a pretty sight to see him as they tied him in the guillotine. He was a wretched coward, and writhed and howled in agony; but when he was once tied, we made sure work of him, and the coward's head was soon lying in the sawdust basket."

"My God!" said Stewart, "this old jailer takes a pride in his profession. Let us leave this place. A streak of light has broken in on our search. The path of the murderer has been found, and that path has led him to a fearful death. We have yet to learn more, ere the streak of light shall have become the clearness of noonday."

Then taking their leave, the garrulous old French jailer bowed them out of the prison, wearied, worried, and discomfited with their search.

From the description of the prisoner given by the jailer, Wattie had no hesitation in recognising the stranger who had been his passenger from Ardmillan. But although the man was in all probability the same, the story of his sister might be strictly true. There was a chance, but only a chance, of the woman being Kitty Sinclair.

As they walked towards the quay where the Jack lay moored, Stewart told Wattie Martin the whole story of his supernatural visitation. The result was that they determined to lay the contents of the sealed packet before Montgomery, give him the result of their united information, and have a thorough consultation. On reaching here Stewart descended to the cabin for the packet. What was his surprise to find that it was gone from the place in which he had secreted it— gone—stolen—vanished as thoroughly as the vision had vanished before. The proofs absent, he could not expect anyone to place credence in the story of his awful visitation. In one moment he realised his position. He rushed wildly up the companion ladder from the cabin, angry and mortified at his own conduct, and tottered against the gunwale of the vessel.

# CHAPTER XI

## WANTED – A CLUE

At first it was the intention of Samuel Stewart to arouse all in the ship. The packet was corporeal. He had held it in his grasp. Although it had almost been handed to him by a spirit, the packet itself was by no means spiritual. Of this there could be no doubt. On further consideration, however, he would wait until the morning. To make any fuss over a bundle of letters would do no good. It took him a full hour to come to this decision, and when he had made up his mind he did the most prudent thing he could under the circumstances—that is to say, he went to bed to think it out.

As we have mentioned in a previous chapter, the cabin of the Jack o Lantern contained two miserable sleeping boxes. In one of these lay the young Earl tossing in an unquiet slumber. The other one was occupied by Stewart. When he had managed to retire, the swinging of the boat rocked him as if he had been in a cradle. He was soon asleep in spite of the uneasiness of his friend. Towards the morning he was aroused by a great noise in his cabin. When he raised his head he saw—not a ghost, but what at first sight might easily have passed for one—the face of the Earl, pale and cadaverous. His eyes stared wildly and yet vacantly. He was babbling some romantic nonsense. Stewart was thoroughly aroused. He saw at once that Hugh Montgomery was ill. To spring from his narrow bed and perform his toilet was a work not occupying long. A medical man was brought from St. Malo who pronounced Montgomery's illness to be fever, and forthwith began to extract blood from a too bloodless body. Weeks might elapse before he would be able to hold a rational conversation. The consultation was thus deferred. The double mystery was deepening at the very moment it seemed to grow clearer. There was no doubt that a consultation with the Earl would have brought about important results. But a conversation was out of the question. They must wait and wait. In the uncertain future something might happen which would lead Stewart to discovery.

That day was a miserable one to all on board the Jack. In the afternoon the Earl was removed to the house of a friend on shore, and there was nothing for it but that the Jack o Lantern should return home. As for Stewart, he was determined not to leave his friend. They agreed, however, that the Jack was to remain at St. Malo for a few days longer in the hope that a favourable change might appear in the patient. In the meantime Stewart spent the time attending on his sick friend, and Wattie passed the days as well as he could—with an eye to future business of a contraband nature. Again Fortune favoured them when they least expected her smiles. The blind goddess remained true to her traditions. They stumbled on a fresh clue. Strolling one day along the street in the company of the medical man, they met a gentleman whom the doctor introduced as M. Guigot, the Marechal of the town. He was a short, square man, sprightly in mind, plethoric in body, and kindly in disposition. His laugh had the natural ring of the true Frenchman. Before they parted, the Marechal invited them to spend the evening in his hospitable mansion.

In the evening Stewart, Wattie, and the doctor met again at the house of M. Guigot. Stewart, as we have stated, had spent a considerable portion of his early life on the Continent. He was consequently quite at home in a French conversation. As for Wattie, whatever patois he had acquired in his trading expeditions, it was almost useless to him in enabling him to understand the polite language of La Belle France. However, the difficulty was considerably smoothed by the patience of Stewart, who considerately acted as interpreter to his friend.

M. Guigot talked like—a Frenchman—and told many a story of his own experience. His conversation was most entertaining.

"I am doubly delighted to have met you," said he, "for it so happens that Englishmen are very scarce in this city. There is a document in my custody at present of a very extraordinary character, which I wish you could translate for me."

Stewart told him that he would only be too happy to be of any service to him in that way, and inquired the nature of the document to which he referred.

"I really am unable to say," said Guigot, "It was found among the papers of a prisoner who was executed about a fortnight ago for murder; but there are none of us here who can really make anything out of it. I should tell you that in the early part of my life," continued the Marechal, "I resided for about five years in England, and although I did not make much progress in the language, I learned enough to enable me to say that the document I am about to show you is written in very strange English."

Without further preface the Marechal arose and, crossing the room to a bureau (which Stewart could not help remarking was almost a facsimile of the antique piece of furniture in Kate Savage's bedroom) he took from a drawer a small piece of paper. It was neatly folded and tied with a piece of string. He reached it over to Stewart.

The old bureau, the folded packet tied with the string, all struck Stewart as more than coincidences. The last time he had stood beside a bureau of that kind he had taken therefrom a similarly folded paper tied with a similar string. His hand trembled as he undid the knots and opened the confession of the murderer; the same one, evidently, whose tortures and death had been so graphically described by the garrulous jailer.

In anxious silence they awaited the discovery. Was their labour ended? Did the small packet in the hand of Stewart contain the information they had sought so eagerly?

The last knot was unloosed. The paper was shaken from its fold. They found bitter disappointment. The paper contained an unintelligible crowding of letters.

They tried to unravel the new mystery. Its meaning was still hidden. The secret of search was a secret as before.

Mechanically Stewart asked permission to copy the document, a permission cheerfully granted. Taking a pocket-book from his pocket book he wrote it down. We here transcribe a portion.

### TO THE FRIENDS OF K—— S——. MY CONFESSION.

"Ov dwiyi kelveyyouly xickw dwi isi uv els oai kwu kel xiet dwij xiet. O uj kiltajlat modzns dwuaqw O texi lud kulviyy ud. Dwi kxoji vux hwoku O ej balojwit oy jud js voxyd uli. Dwi pxati uv Ycidxake wey iykabit ji; endwuaqw O wefi kujjoddit jaxtix vux wix yeci K—— S—— cluhy enn. Ywi honn kuxxupuxedi js ku viyyoul."

"It is no wonder," said Stewart sadly smiling as he tossed away the scribble, "that your English scholars were unable to read this gibberish. It is evidently the raving of some lunatic."

But is there not some meaning lying hid beneath it?" said the doctor, as he scanned the writing.

"Oh, doubtless if we had the key to it, but where is that to be found, besides is it worth the trouble? It is probably some trick on the part of the condemned man."

"You are right, indeed," said the Marechal, "but yet it might contain some great political secret."

"It is much more likely to contain some criminal secret," said Stewart, "what think you, Wattie?"

"A think it's a' nonsense, but mebbe some o' the learned bodies aboot hame cud mak somethin' oot o' it."

"What was the appearance of this extraordinary man, Marechal?" asked Stewart.

"Tall, thin, dark, but well-looking, and—yes I think he had lost a finger from his right hand—But what ails you, Mr. Stewart?"

"My dream!" said Stewart, seizing the writing again, and eagerly scanning it.

"What's it aboot, Mr. Stewart," said Wattie, "d'ye think a pair sailor frae Loch Cowan can un'erstand that jobberin' o' you an' the Frenchman?"

Stewart translated it, and asked Wattie if he recognised the writer.

"The vera man, the vera man," said Wattie. "A min' weel givin' three fingers o' his cloot a squeeze whun he tell't me he was nae gauger. A wish noo A had squeezed it aff him a' thegither."

"It must be the same," said Stewart. "He has undoubtedly murdered one girl and carried off the other. See, here, are her initials—K—— S——. Kitty Sinclair. My poor Kitty! Where is she now?

The scribbling of the criminal was indeed a prize. Oh, that he had a clue or key to this mystic writing! Oh, that he had the packet of letters found in the bureau in Sketrick that he might compare the writing! But, alas! this satisfaction was denied him.

With that pocketbook in his pocket containing the writing purporting to be a confession, they strode moodily shorewards.

There was little conversation between Wattie and Stewart. Each was busy with his own thoughts.

Oh for a key or clue by which he might discover the meaning of the strange words! Stewart tried every language that he knew. Latin, English, Spanish, Italian—it was none of them. He turned and twisted the letters in every direction, but he could make no sense of them at all. He felt there was nothing for it but patience and study. Kate Sinclair's life depended on it perhaps, and should he not work hard to undo, as far as possible, the deeds of villainy committed by this wretch. Perhaps even now he was too late. Kate Sinclair may have been murdered too. Such were the thoughts that urged him on to action, and in the end he was not disappointed. But we must not anticipate the strange events which are yet to be recorded in our history.

# CHAPTER XII

## THE RIDDLE READ

"There are men—doctors—who would keep him here for a month. They would blister him. They would bleed him, and they would make him very much like a sardine."

It was the doctor who spoke.

"I suppose you mean they would cure him," said Stewart, smiling at the energy of the little doctor, who, however, proceeded without paying any attention to the interruption.

"But I would not keep him here. I would not bleed him nor blister him, nor what you call cure him. I shall send him home—to his native country—to get well. You shall see him well in Ireland. He shall go.'

This news came upon Stewart with a crash. Already he had made arrangements for following up the career of the murderer. Wattie was equally determined. The fate of Kitty Sinclair must be unravelled. They had promised to bring home good tidings to Pat Savage of Portneferry. It was hard to be called upon to relax their efforts. Show a greyhound a hare and restrain it. Turn a cat from a mouse she is torturing in the corner. Take the food from a hungry man, and to some extent you will evoke a repetition of the conduct of the crew of the Jack, who all counted upon a reward. Kitty Sinclair had been known to them all. Was she not the daughter of one of themselves, who lost his life while preserving theirs? It was hard to go, and yet it was wrong to stay. They might sacrifice his life by remaining. So said the leech. They might leave her destitute in a foreign land by departing. It ended, however, by the little doctor winning the day. They made preparations for departure. Before nightfall they were most eager to be gone.

Meanwhile Stewart worked assiduously all day at the cipher, for on the morrow they were to depart. It proved to be one of those mystic scrolls in which people of those days often hid secrets which appeared to them to be of importance. His great object was to find the key of the cipher, feeling now assured that it contained information as to the whereabouts of Kitty Sinclair of Ringhaddie, who had been missing for so long. He had counted all the characters in the mysterious writing, and in the portion of it we have given, it stood thus—

The letter '**i**' occurred 35 times.
The letter '**o**' occurred 15 times.
The letter '**x**' occurred 16 times.
The letter '**e**' occurred 14 times.
The word '**dwi**' occurred 3 times.
The letter '**i**' therefore occurred the oftenest.

He then counted a page of print and found that in English the letter *e* occurred far more frequently than any other in the alphabet. He therefore came to the conclusion that '**i**' the cipher stood for *e*. Of the words in the page of print in which he counted, be found that the word *the* occurred most frequently, and finding that '**dwi**' occurrs more than any other, he set it down accordingly as the word *the*. He now knew three letters—**d** in the cipher corresponding to *t*, **w** to *h*, and **i** to *e*. The word '**ywi**' near the last, he translated as *she*, and thus held that **y** corresponded to *s*. Taking the second word in the writing, '**dwiyi**,' he knew it must stand for *these*, and so he, proceeded through a laborious calculation, but which at every step grew easier, until he had the whole writing translated. It stood thus:

# THE MYSTERY OF STRANGFORD LOUGH

## THE LAST CONFESSION OF H. K.

"If these confessions reach the eye of anyone who can read them, let them, let them read. I am condemned justly, though I dare not confess it. The crime for which I am to be punished is not my first one. The bride of Sketrick has escaped me, although I have committed murder for her sake. K—S—knows all; she will corroborate my confession. On the sixth day of December, I waited at Ardmillan, till the carriage came up. The sponge was ready and the sleeping mixture prepared. When she left the coach it was placed under the seat. On the way home the murder was committed and then the abduction. Why do those eyes still haunt me? Even now steeped in crime as I am, I can hardly bear the recollection. May God forgive me."

Such was the interpretation of this mysterious document. It did not, it is true, give him the information so much desired, yet it added another link to the chain of evidence, and was corroborated and explained in many parts by the curious dream that the young Earl related to his friend ere their departure from Sketrick Castle. But the truth was still hidden, and all was uncertainty. One victim, Miss Savage, reposed in peace in the lovely graveyard of Killinchy, but where was Kitty Sinclair!—They had come to save her. Their task was still undone, and they were obliged to return home defeated, and with no certain news. The cypher pointed unmistakeably to her; yet where was she to be found!

One or two things troubled Stewart much. It had been apparent to him that a coolness had been growing between the Earl and himself. As a tender nurse Stewart had sat by the sick bed for many a night and had carefully attended to him during the day. He could not say that the Earl was ungrateful. Hugh de Montgomery often spoke to his faithful friend in terms of endearment and true gratitude. Yet there was something—a forbidden ground—a sore spot between them that Stewart found with great sorrow.

The Jack and her crew had determined to sail on the morrow. They would abandon the search for the lady. The Earl had so far recovered that he had been able to return to his friend on board the Jack. On this evening he had, with the assistance of his friend, been able to sit on the deck aft. Stewart sat beside him. They were conversing, but not with that freedom they once would have talked. They had been speaking of the prospects of a fine passage, and a long pause succeeded.

"Samuel," said the Earl in the peevish fretful tone he spoke in now, "I can never forget your kindness to me as I lay ill, but I am not satisfied altogether with you."

"In what way, sir? I am sure I have striven to return your friendship by the best services I could perform."

"You have kept news from me that I should have known."

"I?"

"You have followed out your own plan of detection without consulting me when I would have given you material assistance."

It was useless for Stewart to assert that anything ever he knew he had either told him, or intended to tell him, when something prevented him. The Earl continued—

"I was more interested than you could have been in the discovery of Kitty Sinclair and in the discovery of that crime on my poor, poor—" then he broke down.

"I assure you, sir," said Stewart, "I know of nothing I could have told you in which you could have given me any assistance."

"Speak the truth, Samuel Stewart. It ill betides you to speak false to a man who is unable to chastise you. Why did you not show me that?" Here the Earl placed upon the table the incidental packet which had once been in Stewart's possession, and which he had lost so suddenly. Had one of Jove's thunderbolts been hurled from high Olympus and shivered the mainmast of the vessel, Stewart could hardly have looked more terrified. The appearance of that innocent packet had more effect upon him than the rude words of his companion a few minutes before. He was positively struck dumb.

"Where did you get those letters, Samuel Stewart?" said the Earl.

"In the black bureau in the room in which I slept in Sketrick Castle," he answered as, half-frightened at their sudden re-appearance, he eyed the mystic packet.

"And did you retain them in your possession, knowing them, or at least a portion of them, to have been letters from me to Miss Savage?"

"I did."

"Why did you not return my letters to me?"

Stewart explained how he had intended to do so, but feared to revive the great sorrow in the mind of his friend, and yet considered it more prudent to bring them with him. By that means he might show them to the Earl again, or by the other packet seek for a clue.

"Did you read them?" asked Hugh de Montgomery.

"No, sir, I did not read them, save the awful superscription I read none of them: Have you read them."

"All."

"Have you read the sealed packet which was not to be shewn to you until—until—the time came?"

"I have read them all."

"Do you know the writer?"

"I do. Herbert Cassidy. She has often told me how he

followed her with proposals of marriage. I never liked him."

His letter had been unopened, I think."

"His letters had been unopened."

"Can you assign a reason?"

"None, except that she had accepted him."

Then Samuel Stewart did a strange action. He walked deliberately up to the bows of the smack, sat down on a coil of rope—rose up and slowly returned to the place where the Earl sat watching him.

# CHAPTER XIII

## THE HORIZON CLEARS

When Samuel Stewart returned to the Earl's side, he asked him a straight sharp question. It was this—

"Does that packet—I mean the packet of Herbert Cassidy's letters—contain anything you don't understand?"

"Nothing."

Stewart continued his slow march round the deck of the Jack. As he returned from his round he had another question.

"Do you suspect any one?"

"I do."

"Cassidy?"

"Cassidy."

Next time it was the Earl who put the questions.

"Do you know him?" said he.

"I never saw him," replied Stewart.

"But you have heard of him?"

"Yes."

"And suspect him?"

"How many fingers has he on his right hand?"

"Three. He lost one in a duel."

"I know that he is the murderer and the abductor," replied Stewart slowly and calmly.

"How do you know that," said the other, becoming in his turn excited.

"Hush!" said Stewart, "and you will hear all. We cannot afford to send you back into a brain fever."

"Well?"

"I have her words, and his handwriting."

"How—where—tell me!"

Samuel Stewart took from his pocket an old well-worn pocket book, and looking over it selected two slips of paper. He laid one of them before the Earl, simply saying—

"Her words."

Hugh de Montgomery looked at the writing. The evening was wearing apace, but there was sufficient light to enable him to read these words—

> *"Keep back, Hugh—oh take your hand from my throat! What, a knife—I tell you I am another's."*

The Earl sat looking at the writing a long time. His eyes floated in mist. He was roused by the other handing him another paper, saying as before, shortly and quietly—

"His handwriting."

The paper contained the confession of H. C. and the translation of it side by side.

"How does this prove it, Samuel," said the Earl, beginning to feel like a child before the strong-mindedness of Stewart.

"Let me see one of his letters and let us compare the writing."

The letter was opened. The manuscript of the confession was laid beside the manuscript of a letter. Every turn and outline agreed. The same hand had penned both. That was evident.

"You know everything," said the Earl, "where is he now? Oh, that I had strength to arise and slay him."

"There is no occasion. He is dead."

"Dead!"

"Dead by the guillotine."

Then he told the story, as we have striven to tell it, of the garrulous French jailer; of the urbane Marechal M. Guigot, till the fading day melted into night, and the stars shone downwards with pure cold ray.

The Earl listened attentively to the narration of Samuel Stewart; but as his narrative embraced the different matter which we have already narrated to our readers at some length, we are not going to weary their patience by a repetition of it.

"I wish very much, Stewart," said he, when the latter had finished, "that you had told me all this before. I believe if I had been possessed of your information I could have made this discovery perhaps in time to see the scoundrel expiating his crime. Your narrative recalls to my mind an event with which you are not acquainted, but which I may tell you now. We were sitting—Miss Savage and I—in one of the rooms of Sketrick Castle, a few evenings before the day for which our marriage had been arranged. Some sudden weakness, perhaps stupor, perhaps faintness, seized her. She fainted in my arms, and was removed to her own room. When she had recovered I was admitted to see her, and recollect her making use of an observation which has haunted me ever since. It was this—'As if it were my last command, I charge you that if anything happens to me you must look in my —.' She stopped here. She did not tell me where I was to look. When I spoke of it again she laughed me off. She was fickle, but she was ill at the time and but lately recovered from her fainting fit."

"Of course you know now where she wished you to look!"

"Yes, I know now, thanks to you, the bureau in the very room in which we then stood. But there was something else. She had a vision of her fate in that trance. The old nurse who had been servant in the family for many years heard her use some strange words that she could not then understand. They seem quite plain."

"What were they?" said Stewart, in his turn becoming interested.

The Earl produced a pocket-book, and selecting one paper from several, laid it before Stewart. He read as follows—

*"Keep back, Hugh!—Oh, take your hand from my throat. What, a knife!—I tell you I am another's."*

It was the copy of the words used by Kate taken by Hugh de Montgomery from the nurse's copy.

"I see it all," said Stewart. "Read those words in connection with the confession of Cassidy, with the terrible reality you saw in the coach, and with the terrible vision I saw in her bedroom."

"Do you know, Samuel, I begin to think with the ancients that warnings are sent to us many a time for our guidance, but we are too proud or too ignorant to take advantage of them."

"There is no doubt," Stewart replied, "that Miss Savage must have had some indication of the Future in her trance. There is more than imagination in all this."

"Yes, Samuel, it puts me in mind of a quotation from one of the plays of that fellow—Shakespeare—who made such a name in London a few years ago. 'There are more things in Heaven and earth, Horatio, than are dreamt of in your philosophy.'"

As they rose to retire they were greeted by a hearty shout from Wattie Martin, who came on board.

He beckoned Stewart to come. They moved into the shadow of the deckhouse, and stood there for minute. When they emerged Stewart said—

"You may speak freely, Wattie, what you have told me. The Earl knows all. The mystic packet has appeared. Our patient had it all the time—"

"And it was the shock of getting it," said the patient, "that made me ill. I can stand anything now—pray go on."

"Weel, sir," said Wattie, giving his trousers the customary hitch, "ye see A aye suspected that that deevil wi' three fingers that A brocht ower frae Ardmillen, was the ane we were in search o'. Weel, as he was deed, A made it my business the night tae luk a wee bit after the leddy. Sae I traced her frae ane place to anither an' yin o' them puddin-faced men 'John Darmes'. First she had been here, and then she had been there, trying tae slip awa' frae him. It wad hae been ower much for her, puir thing, had John Darmes no arreested my three-fingered friend. Whun he was caught she gaed clean awa. No a ane in St. Malo has heerd o' her for the last month, an' A'm thinkin' it's as like as not that Kitty Sinclair is hame by the auld rigs o' Killinchy by this time."

"Give me your hand, Wattie"

They grasped hands.

"Can you steal a march on the old 'John Darmes' at the fort, as you call them, and start wi' the Jack o Lantern right off?"

"Aye. deed A can dae that, sir. A hae din it afore, an' can dae it again."

The two passengers descended to their cabin.

Wattie roused his men, and in half-an-hour the anchor was tripped, and the Jack o Lantern was sliding down on the current past the fort at the entrance to the harbour.

On the next morning when the Earl appeared on deck accompanied by Stewart a great change was observable on him. The bloom of returning strength was on his cheek. The light of health was in his eye. The brain fever, induced by his suddenly seeing his old love-letters and the letters of Cassidy, had spent itself. She had been dead to him as an angel—the angel of his love—the ideal of his ardent youth. Thus while to the world she was dead she was doubly dead to him. Though the time had come, indicated by her spirit at which the packet might be shown to her lover, still the sight of the letters carried a shock terrible to bear.

On the passage home Stewart told him all he had known, which, after all was nothing until supplemented by the knowledge of the Earl. When they two had put their heads together the truth came forth.

It was a pleasant and rapid passage. Now and then they met a Dutch lugger looking for reprisals, and escaped at their heels. They were too eager to return to Portneferry to engage in any fighting now, even with the hope of making so profitable a prize as a Dutchman in these times. On the following day (Monday) they had to cross the Bar and make the old anchorage of Ballyhendry—this time, however, with nothing contraband on board. It did not for the moment occur to them that the Monday was a day of fasting in all Christian lands. It was Easter Monday. Already the horns of the ford, like arms, were open to receive them into the fair bosom of the County Down.

# CHAPTER XIV

## CONCLUSION

The little village of Portaferry is situated on the Northern shores of the Ford of Strangford, or as it was called at the time of our story, and for many years afterwards, Strongford. It is picturesquely surrounded by hills, and was then the residence of a number of gentlemen.

It is the morning of Easter Monday. The Jack o Lantern is riding safely at her anchorage. Her arrival has been duly reported to Mr. Patrick Savage, and as the day is a holiday, the arrival is opportune. Immediately on being informed of the arrival of the little vessel, Mr. Savage despatched a boat, and requested all on board to meet him in his demesne at noon. It was fully that time before they were ready to leave the ship.

As they sailed up the old quay of Portaferry, a great crowd was gathered on the shore, and, amid cheering they little understood the Earl of Strangford, Moore, and Wattie leaped ashore. Patrick Savage was there to welcome them, and conduct them through the gates of his demesne to the hollow, a short distance from the entrance gate, where the men of the Jack had stood when he addressed them on the eve of their expedition. The grounds here were thronged with people, who shouted and cheered lustily as they approached, to the no small amazement of the voyagers. A little platform was raised on the western side of the basin, to which Mr. Savage conducted the three worthies, while the rest of the sailors scattered through the crowd, and joined in the chorus of cheers that rang through the old woods of Portaferry and across to Strangford town.

When silence was obtained, Mr. Patrick Savage rose to address them.

"My men," said he, "you have returned. It is true you have not brought back her whom you went to rescue, nor can you compel the grave to yield up the dead. But ere you went away, I promised that the day of your return should be signalled by a great gathering of people and much feasting. I have kept my word. The people are gathered. The feast is being prepared. My desire is that this feast shall be perpetuated through all posterity by being celebrated every Easter Monday on this spot, and that every fair lady who graces it with her presence shall submit to be kissed by any of the sterner sex that may demand that boon. I have sought for a name by which this place shall be known in all generations, but I have found none so worthy to my mind as that of the brave man who conducted the villain from these shores and brought tears to the maids of Strongford, and afterwards by going in search of the murderer, replaced those tears by smiles. Need I tell you that man is Wattie Martin? Let this spot be called the 'Walter' after him from this day, and let no plough ever break its surface. Now let those approach this platform whose chief business it is to be present at our celebration."

There was a great cheering and hurrahing—a motion of the crowd as if some persons were forcing their way through it; meanwhile the Earl and his party stood in mute surprise gazing at one another. The events were so rapid, so unexplained, they have believed them real.

At last out from the crowd into the open space, stepped a venerable old man, and a fair girl leaning on his arm. One glance was sufficient.

"Hugh!"

"Kate!"

Had Kate Savage arisen from the dead?—Yes, there she stood!

# THE MYSTERY OF STRANGFORD LOUGH

In another moment Hugh de Montgomerie and Kate Savage were locked in each other's arms, and Philip Savage, Pat Savage, Moore, and Walter were shaking hands with everybody.

"Now," roared Pat Savage, the first kiss has been given on the Walter. Boys, where are you?" Then followed a scene of kissing and shouting, cheering and dancing, and making merry, that youth and age alike forgot their toil.

Who can describe the happy scene in the Walter of Portaferry demesne! Games, of all sorts were instituted which to this day have been handed down to posterity, and still may be seen performed with religious zeal on the part of the demesne still called by the name of Walter Martin. Foremost among these rights celebrated to this day is that of it being compulsory on every lady who enters the ring to give a kiss to the lowest churl who may demand it. Perhaps this condition was not exacted? Gentle reader, you may trust the brave lads of Portaferry to being dead to such a guerdon. There were races instituted, and other sports that still live to speak of olden times, when the name of Wattie Martin has almost been forgotten. Long may these happy scenes prevail at Portaferry to tell of days gone by.

Then came the feast, to which, let us hope, all parties did ample justice. At least many a ringing cheer resounded over the waters of the lough, and many a maiden's eye glistened with delight as the fair young Kate leaned on her lover's arm, and walked among the throng that merry Easter Monday. And many a young man's look rested lovingly and proudly on the manly figure of Hugh de Montgomerie as he moved among the merry crowd with his lost bride upon his arm.

The story of what befell Kate Savage is easily told, but the mystery of Strangford Lough is still a mystery as deep as when two hundred years ago the village gossips told the story. Although two hundred years and more have fled, the gloom is as dark and impenetrable as ever. Kate remembered getting into the coach at Ardmillan, after the horseshoeing operation had been completed. She felt a heavy, sickening smell within the coach, and she remembered no more till she found herself disguised in other garments in the cabin of the smuggling smack. Herbert Cassidy, an Englishman, whom she had met on several occasions, and who had pestered her with letters of attachment, was her jailer. By him she was taken to Saint Malo. Here he had tried to coerce her into marriage, but she resisted all his efforts, and eventually she managed to escape from him. Having made good her flight, she concealed herself in the house of a poor woman for a fortnight, undergoing many privations and much distress on account of her friends at home. By means of her jewellery, with which she parted by degrees, she at last, using great caution, reached her own old home in the bosom of Lough Cowan, where she had been living for some time before the Jack o Lantern arrived. She had tried to communicate with the Earl, but she knew not his whereabouts. Postal communication was then a thing of the future, and consequently she sat bewailing the absence of her lover in Sketrick while he, having given her up as dead—murdered by the hand of an assassin he did not know—was searching for Kitty Sinclair in the purlieus of a French city.

Poor Kitty Sinclair. In the quiet graveyard of Killinchy she still rests the innocent victim of Cassidy's brutal passion. It is supposed, but mystery enwraps it all, that the assassin, presuming upon the likeness that existed between Miss Savage and Kitty Sinclair, had, after making both insensible changed the clothes of the girls, placed Kitty in the coach, and committed the foul-crime which we have described. This supposition was borne out by the fact that the face was intentionally mutilated, so as to prevent recognition by even the most intimate friends of Miss Savage. This supposition was borne out by the production of the clothes in which Miss Savage found herself on board the boat. They were proved to have been the clothes of Kitty Sinclair when she was last seen on her way to school at Carrickfergus, whither she was being sent by Pat Savage, of Portnaferry, who took a great interest in the girl on account of the remarkable likeness between her and her niece. None of the confederates in the murder or abduction were ever discovered, although there must have been several.

The object of the murder of Kitty Sinclair was obviously to throw off suspicion until the murderer would get far off with his fair prize.

Be it as it may, however, it still remains a mystery, and by the old ruins of Sketrick Castle the tourist will find many a hoary-headed resident who still speaks fondly of the young Mistress of Sketrick in the olden time, and the sad death of Kitty Sinclair, of Ringhaddie, whose name still lives in that beautiful and fertile district.

Samuel Stewart settled down in Sketrick in the home of his fathers. His health did not permit him to embark in the profession which he had adopted. However, being of an unambitious and gentle temper, he enjoyed his life perhaps, by the homely old shores as much as if he had come to occupy the highest position in the land. He became the founder of a family whose descendants are still on the island of Sketrick, and who still cherish the recollection of their simple ancestor.

Walter Martin continued his old trade till age and infirmities laid him to rest in the old graveyard of Killyleagh, a revered and venerable grandfather. His descendants still live round his native village, and more than one yet glories in the name of Wattie.

Sir Philip Savage, of Sketrick, left his castle shortly after the marriage of his daughter, and resided with them in Ringhaddie till a green old age. He was the last tenant of Sketrick

Castle, which, from the day he left till the present, has been slowly sinking into decay. Now only four bare walls remain of the once glorious Sketrick.

Hugh de Montgomerie and Kate Savage were married by the good old Livingstone in the lowly meetinghouse of Killinchy, as they often wished and prayed for.

A short time after the celebration of the marriage they went to reside at the Castle of Ringhaddie. They remained there together, blessed by a numerous and happy family, until, by the death of her father, the estates devolved upon him.

Sir Hugh Montgomery, Earl of Mount Alexander, then removed to Newtown. It is related in the Montgomery manuscripts that "in Summer, 1608, some of the Priory walls were roofed and fitted for his lady and children and servants (which were many) to live in," and in a short time afterwards "the rest of these walls and other large additions of a gate-house and office-houses, which made three sides of a quadrangle (the Scottish side of the Church being contiguous, made the fourth side)." The buildings and the establishment became princely in dimensions and management. This mansion, Newtown House, was afterwards burned in 1664 and on its site Colville House was erected, which met with a similar fate.

In the year 1636 Sir Hugh Montgomery erected in the centre of his courtyard, in the top of a vault, the structure now called the Old Cross. It was built to commemorate his marriage with the fair Kate, although the reason of erection appears to have been soon forgotten, and to have been used for other purposes. For in "A Description of the Barony called the Ards, dedicated unto Patrick Savage of Portaferry, Esq., by William Montgomery, Esq., Anno Domini Christ 1701," it is described thus:—"In ye middle of this fabrick upon ye vault aforesd, stands a pillar of hewn stones of eight squares, about twenty foot high, with a lyon seyant on ye topp. This whole piece of work is called ye Mercat Cross; whence are made public (with ye town solemnitys) all proclamations that come from our chief governor, and their own town business which needs an outcry. The body of this building (which is seen of four streets) hath ye King's arms fronting to ye great street, etc., etc."

The pile of that old cross still remains; and with it the name of Hugh Montgomery will be associated as long as this reverend monument stands in the good old town of Newtown.

And thus endeth all that poet or historian can write or knoweth of

THE MYSTERY OF STRANGFORD LOUGH.

# GLOSSARY

| | |
|---|---|
| **A** | I |
| **a ane** | one (a one). *"No **a ane** in St. Malo has heerd o' her for the last month"* |
| **a'** | all. *"It was weel for us puir fishin' bodies that we were **a'** in afore"* |
| **a' thegither** | altogether. |
| **A'm** | I'm |
| **aboot** | about |
| **aff** | off. |
| **afore** | before. |
| **aften** | often. |
| **ails** | is wrong with. *"What **ails** ye, Master Stewart? Is there ocht wrang?"* |
| **ain** | own. *"It was my **ain** son, yer reverence, that drove her on the wy tae Cumer"* |
| **airt** | part (of the world). *"Ay, mony o' them, the name's common aneuch in this **airt**"* |
| **amang** | among. |
| **an'** | and. |
| **ane** | one. |
| **aneuch** | enough. *"Ay, mony o' them, the name's common **aneuch** in this airt"* |
| **anither** | another. |

81

# GLOSSARY

**arreested**    arrested.

**auch**    oh! (exclamation). *"**Auch** an' this was sad news aboot Miss Savage!"*

**auld**    old.

**ava**    at all. *"She was aye sayin' when she got the chance that she wusnae his sister **ava**"*

**awa, awa'**    away. *"Whun he was caught she gaed clean **awa**"*

**ay**    yes. *"'Oh, **ay**, man,' said Jamey, 'they haenae till rin the risk o' bein' drooned on sic a nicht as this'"*

**aye**    always. *"She was **aye** sayin' when she got the chance that she wusnae his sister **ava**"*

**baith**    both.

**barnacles**    brent geese. *"That's Kirkcubben, sir, and yonner whaar ye see the spot o' lan' comin' oot intil the sea is the best place for a shot at the **barnacles** and widgeons aboot a' this airt"*

**bein'**    being'. *"'Oh, ay, man,' said Jamey, 'they haenae till rin the risk o' **bein'** drooned on sic a nicht as this'"*

**betther**    better.

**black**    bad. *"'Oh, minister, dear,' she said excitedly, 'this is a **black** day for Killinchy'"*

**black-avised**    dark complexioned. *"A had an inklin' that yon **black-avised** fellow an' his sister wuz nae guid"*

# GLOSSARY

**bodies**      people. *"It was weel for us puir fishin' bodies that we were a' in afore"*

**bonnie, bonny**      pretty.

**brauken**      broken.

**brocht**      brought.

**by an' bye**      eventually. *"But by an' bye it turned oot mair."*

**ca'ed**      called. *"She wuz a woman that he aye ca'ed his sister"*

**cam'**      came.

**cam' on**      started (came on). *"Ay. Sir, rough aneuch. It was weel for us puir fishin' bodies that we were a' in afore it cam' on."*

**canna**      can't.

**Carrick**      Carrickfergus. *"She haesna been heard tell o' since she left tae gang tae Carrick"*

**cloot**      paw. *"A min' weel givin' three fingers o' his cloot a squeeze whun he tell't me he was nae gauger"*

**compleen**      complain.

**Corncat**      Scottish mythical spirit among the corn. *"Mr. Cathcart, commonly known as Dr. Corncat, was the only doctor in the neighbourhood"*

**cud**      could.

**Cumer, Cummer**      Comber. *"It was my ain son, yer reverence, that drove her on the wy tae Cumer"*

# GLOSSARY

| | |
|---|---|
| **cumin'** | coming. |
| **d'ye** | do you. |
| **dae** | do. *"I wadnae **dae** muckle hairm when ane o' them is near han'"* |
| **daurna** | daren't. |
| **de'il, devil** | devil. |
| **deed** | dead. *"Weel, tae be plain wi' ye, he is **deed**— **deed** as a maggot, docther"* |
| **Deed!** | Indeed! *"**Deed**, sir, if I can rightly tell ye. She wuz a woman that he aye ca'ed his sister."* |
| **depen's** | depends. |
| **didnae** | didn't. |
| **din** | done. *"Aye. deed A can dae that, sir. A hae **din** it afore, an' can dae it again"* |
| **dinna'** | don't. |
| **disnae** | doesn't. |
| **dochters** | daughters. *"Frae Ballydorn tae Ballyquinton there wusnae a dry e'e amang the **dochters** of the shore"* |
| **docther** | doctor. *"Weel, tae be plain wi' ye, he is deed—deed as a maggot, **docther**"* |
| **doon** | down. |
| **drappin'** | dropping. |
| **drooned** | drowned. |
| **e'e** | eye. *"there wusnae a dry **e'e** amang the dochters of the shore"* |

84

**em**  am. *"richt shair em A aboot that Wullie Sinclair"*

**faither**  father. *"There's 'Lang Tam' and 'Big Johnny'; 'The Fluker,' and 'Auld Robin,' his faither, an' 'Wee Wattie o' the Jack.'"*

**fause**  false. *"The wreckers hae a richt easy wae o' leevin', Jamey: but A canna say A'm in favour o' showin' them fause lichts"*

**fishin' bodies**  fisher-folk.

**fleein'**  flying. *"he observed a muckle bright licht fleein' up an' doon ower the watter"*

**fluker**  fisher of 'flukes' (flounders). *"There's 'Lang Tam' and 'Big Johnny'; 'The Fluker,' and 'Auld Robin,' his faither, an' 'Wee Wattie o' the Jack.'"*

**frae**  from.

**gaed**  went. *"Whun he was caught she gaed clean awa"*

**gang**  go. ***"She haesna been heard tell o' since she left tae gang tae Carrick"***

**gauger**  customs and excise man. *"A min' weel givin' three fingers o' his cloot a squeeze whun he tell't me he was nae gauger"*; *"Every unknown person was a King's bailiff or a gauger"*

**ghaist**  ghost.

**Ghaist Hole**  'The Haunted Pool' (a spot on a creek of Strangford Lough near Comber). *"It was my ain son, yer reverence, that drove her on*

> the wy tae Cumer. An' just as they come by
> the **ghaist hole**—ye ken the **ghaist hole**, yer
> reverence"

**gi'e** — give.

**gled** — glad. *"A'm richt **gled**, sir," said Wattie, "that ye hae been fortunate"*

**gould** — gold. *"Na, na, it's no yer siller A want. Honest folk wunnae tell on their neighbours for the like o' that. Pit up yer **gould**, man."*

**greetin'** — crying, weeping. *"The hale kintra side is just **greetin'** aboot her"*

**Gude** — God. *"**Gude** help them, … **Gude** save us!"*

**guerdon** — reward. *"you may trust the brave lads of Portaferry to being dead to such a **guerdon**"*

**guid** — good.

**hae** — have.

**haesna, haenae** — haven't. *"'Oh, ay, man,' said Jamey, 'they **haenae** till rin the risk o' bein' drooned on sic a nicht as this'"; "She **haesna** been heard tell o' since she left tae gang tae Carrick"*

**hairm** — harm.

**hale** — whole. *"The **hale** kintra side is just greetin' aboot her"*

**hame** — home.

**han'** — hand.

**har'ly** — hardly.

**has** — have. *"Mony an' mony a time **has** we twa*

# GLOSSARY

sailed thegither owre the bonny waters of
Loch Cowan"

**heard tell o'** (no) news about. *"She haesna been **heard tell o'** since she left tae gang tae Carrick"*

**heerd, heered** heard. *"Nay, sir, I niver **heered** his name"*; *"No a ane in St. Malo has **heerd** o' her for the last month"*

**hereaboot** about here. *"Ay, sir; lang aneuch to ken maist folks hereabout"*

**herrin'** herring.

**Hoot** Goodness! (exclamation). *"Hoot, mother, for shame! Tell me how he is?"*

**intil** into. "the spot o' lan' comin' oot **intil** the sea is the best place"

**ir** are. *"**Ir** ye shair thae warhawks **ir** no stirrin' the nicht?"*

**ither** other.

**Jamey** Jim, Jimmy, James.

**jist** just.

**ken** know.

**kep'** **kept.**

**kintra** side countryside. *"The hale **kintra side** is just greetin' aboot her"*

**Kirkcubben** Kircubbin. *"That's **Kirkcubben**, sir, and yonner whaar ye see the spot o' lan' comin' oot intil the sea is the best place for a shot at the barnacles and widgeons aboot a' this airt"*

# GLOSSARY

**Kitty**             Catherine, Kate.

**lan'**              land.

**lang**              long.

**Lang Tam**          'tall' Tom. *"There's **Lang Tam** and 'Big
                      Johnny'; 'The Fluker,' and 'Auld Robin,' his
                      **faither**, an' 'Wee Wattie o' the Jack.'"*

**lassie**            girl.

**learned bodies**    educated people. *"but mebbe some o' the
                      **learned bodies** aboot hame cud mak some-
                      thin' oot o' it"*

**leddy**             lady.

**leevin'**           living. *"The wreckers hae a richt easy wae o'
                      **leevin'**"*

**leevin'**           living (noun). *"rin the risk o' bein' drooned
                      on sic a nicht as this while seekin' an honest
                      **leevin'** frae the sea"*

**licht**             light.

**liker**             more like. *"the people say we are **liker** each
                      other than ever"*

**luk**               look.

**mair**              more.

**maist**             most.

**mak, mak'**         make.

**maun**              **must.** *"Ah, well, A **maun** thole, A **maun**
                      thole!"*

# GLOSSARY

| | |
|---|---|
| **may** | had better, might as well. *"Ye **may** e'en gang back hame again, docther,"* |
| **mebbe** | maybe. |
| **min'** | mind, remember. *"tae nae purpose but tae pit ye in **min'** o' yer young days"*; *"A **min'** weel givin' three fingers o' his cloot a squeeze"* |
| **mony** | many. *"Ay, **mony** o' them, the name's common aneuch in this airt"* |
| **mony a time** | often. |
| **muckle** | much. *"I wadnae dae **muckle** hairm when ane o' them is near han'"* |
| **mune** | moon. *"Wait; the **mune's** cumin' oot"* |
| **mysel'** | myself. |
| **na** | no. *"**Na, na**, it's no yer siller A want"* |
| **nae** | no. *"he tell't me he was **nae** gauger"* |
| **near han'** | nearby. *"I wadnae dae muckle hairm when ane o' them is **near han'**"* |
| **nicht** | night. *"rin the risk o' bein' drooned on sic a **nicht** as this while seekin' an honest leevin' frae the sea"* |
| **niver** | never. |
| **no, no'** | not. *"Ir ye shair thae warhawks ir **no** stirrin' the nicht?"* |
| **noo** | now. |
| **o'** | of. |

**ocht**       anything. *"What ails ye, Master Stewart? Is there **ocht** wrang?"*

**ony**        any.

**onything**   anything.

**oor**        our.

**oot**        out.

**ordinar'**   everyday.

**owre**       over. *"he observed a muckle bright licht flee-in' up an' doon **ower** the watter"*

**pair**       poor. *"d'ye think a **pair** sailor frae Loch Cowan can un'erstand that jobberin'"*

**pit up**     put away. *"Na, na, it's no yer siller A want. Honest folk wunnae tell on their neighbours for the like o' that. **Pit up** yer gould, man."*

**pit ye in min' o'**   remind you. *"tae nae purpose but tae **pit ye in min' o'** yer young days"*

**plain**      straightforward. *"Weel, tae be **plain** wi' ye, he is deed"*

**puir**       poor. *"It was weel for us **puir** fishin' bodies that we were a' in afore"*

**purty**      pretty.

**richt**      right.

**rigs**       ridges, hill-tops. *"it's as like as not that Kitty Sinclair is hame by the auld **rigs** o' Killinchy by this time."*

**rin**        run. *"'Oh, ay, man,' said Jamey, 'they haenae*

| | |
|---|---|
| | *till **rin** the risk o' bein' drooned on sic a nicht as this'"* |
| **Rowting Well** | roaring (like a bull) whirlpool (wheel). *"Already they were nearing the fatal bar that roared and surged with awful noise, while the moaning of the "**Rowting Well**" smote horribly on their ears"* |
| **sae** | so. |
| **shair** | sure. *"Ay, richt **shair** em A aboot that Wullie Sinclair"* |
| **shud** | should. |
| **sic** | such. *"rin the risk o' bein' drooned on **sic** a nicht as this while seekin' an honest leevin' frae the sea"* |
| **siller** | silver, money. *"Na, na, it's no yer **siller** A want. Honest folk wunnae tell on their neighbours for the like o' that. Pit up yer gould, man"* |
| **simmer** | summer. |
| **skule** | school. |
| **stap** | stop, stay. *"Why shud A **stap** them?"* |
| **stappin'** | staying. *"Maybe ye're **stappin'** at the Castle wi' the young Laird o' Hamilton?"* |
| **syne** | since. *"The bonnie lassie that went to skule has no' been heard o' **syne** she left."* |
| **tae** | to. |
| **tak'** | take. |

# GLOSSARY

**Tam**                    Tom.

**tauld**                  told.

**tell on their neighbours**

                           inform.

**tell't**                 told. *"A min' weel givin' three fingers o' his cloot a squeeze whun he **tell't** me he was nae gauger"*

**thae**                   those. *"shot by some o' **thae** murderers they ca' King's men"*

**the nicht**              tonight.

**thegither**              together.

**them**                   those. *"I noticed **them** three fingers the first day I gripped his han'"*

**they ca'**               called, named. *"shot by some o' thae murderers **they ca'** King's men"*

**thocht**                 thought.

**thole**                  endure, put up with (it). *"Ah, well, A maun **thole**, A maun **thole**!"*

**till**                   to. *"'Oh, ay, man,' said Jamey, 'they haenae **till** rin the risk o' bein' drooned on sic a nicht as this'"; "but ye maun see **till** Mr. Savage"*

**tryst**                  appointment, 'date'. *"It was not often she was behindhand in her **trysts** since the early days of courtship, in which it is, we believe, unusual for young ladies to weary out their lovers, and impose taxes upon their patience"*

**twa**    two.

**vera**    very, exact. "*The **vera** man, the **vera** man,*"

**wad**    would.

**wadnae**   wouldn't. "*I **wadnae** dae muckle hairm when ane o' them is near han'*"

**wae**    way. "*The wreckers hae a richt easy **wae** o' leevin'*"

**wae**    with. "*That a' depen's upon what ye want **wae** him*"

**warl'**   world.

**watter**   water. "*he observed a muckle bright licht fleein' up an' doon ower the **watter***"

**Wattie**   Walter. "*Walter (or, as he was commonly called, **Watty**) Martin*"; "*There's 'Lang Tam' and 'Big Johnny'; 'The Fluker,' and 'Auld Robin,' his faither, an' **'Wee Wattie** o' the Jack.'*"

**wee**    little, small.

**weel**    well. "*It was **weel** for us puir fishin' bodies that we were a' in afore*"

**ween**    imagine, suppose. "*there was little thought of it, I **ween**, in that cosy room*"

**wha**    who.

**whaar**   where.

**while**    time. "*Fortune disnae often smile long on us puir fishin' bodies. There's a while o' fillin' an' a **while** o' fastin' wi' tha maist o' us*" (time)

# GLOSSARY

**whun**  when.

**wi'**  with.

**wonderfu'**  wonderful.

**wrang**  wrong. *"What ails ye, Master Stewart? Is there ocht **wrang**?"*

**wudna', wudnae**  wouldn't.

**Wullie**  William, Will.

**wunnae**  won't. *"Honest folk **wunnae** tell on their neighbours for the like o' that"*

**wurnae**  weren't.

**wusnae**  wasn't.

**wuz**  was.

**wy**  way. *"It was my ain son, yer reverence, that drove her on the **wy** tae Cumer"*

**ye**  you.

**ye'll**  you'll.

**yer**  your.

**yersel'**  yourself.

**yin**  one.

**yince**  once. *"A'm richt gled to see ye on board o' the auld Jack **yince** again"*

# GLOSSARY

**yon**

that.

**yonner**

(over) there. *"That's Kirkcubben, sir, and **yonner** whaur ye see the spot o' lan' comin' oot intil the sea is the best place for a shot at the barnacles and widgeons aboot a' this airt"*

Printed in Great Britain
by Amazon